RENOVATING THE HEART OF A BEAST 2

ADDICTED TO A BBW

MASTERPIECE

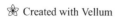 Created with Vellum

SUBSCRIBE

Interested in keeping up with more releases from S.Yvonne Presents? To be notified first on upcoming releases, exclusive sneak peaks, and contest to win prizes. Please subscribe to her mailing list: https://bit.ly/3jKoNbB

SYNOPSIS

SYNOPSIS

The crew is back with a list of problems that need to be fixed! Debo is still struggling mentally with himself, hoping that he doesn't dive too far off the deep end. One of his biggest fears is facing off with himself followed by losing Praylah. Not really understanding himself or his newfound interest in Praylah, he feels himself spiraling. Soulful is finding out that the love of his life has not given him the same loyalty that he has always given. His feelings are twisted, and he finds himself being haunted by his past and the things that has hurt him. Era has finally been blessed with one of her biggest dreams, singing. A huge curveball is thrown her way which lands her right back into the face of Soulful Hurtz. Praylah still battles with depression and her bipolar disorder. Praylah is thrown into more problems with her child's father, Jarei and things suddenly start to take the wrong turn. Relationships are lost, new bonds are made, and love and renovation is in the making for all four individuals. *This book is full of action and drama, raw feelings are exposed, and hearts become broken in hopes to be fixed!*

KEEP IN TOUCH

Subscribe

Interested in keeping up with more of my releases? To be notified first of all my upcoming releases and sneak peeks, please subscribe to my mailing list! https://bit.ly/3AYIwMK
Contact me on any of my social media handles as well!
Facebook- **Authoress Masterpiece & Masterpiece Reads**
Facebook private group for updates- Masterpiece Readers
Instagram- authoress_masterpiece & masterpiece_lgee
Email – masterpiece3541@outlook.com

RECAP

Recap
Debo

"Nigga, why you driving behind the pigs so damn fast! Slow this bitch down!" I looked over at Honor and smirked. She had her feet pressed all hard against the passenger side floor like she was on the driver's side. It looked like she was trying to push down on imaginary brakes. Holding onto her seat belt tight she looked over at me like she was scared. Shit was comical as fuck, I accelerated higher and sped up.

"Chill the fuck out, they going fast, so I'm going the same speed as them. How can they pull me over when I'm behind them. They speed I speed." I turned the music up and switched lanes, following what the cops did. I was in a rush to go break a niggas face in.

Niggas knew that Honor was my General, head bitch in charge. I had too much going on mentally, legally, and illegally to hold niggas nuts and guide them along the way.

"You know I handled that nigga, right?" Honor turned my music down. "Why the fuck you keep playing this old slow

ass song." I shrugged off her question. Smokey Robinson's "The Agony For The Ecstasy" was one of my favorite songs. I usually listened to the shit to calm my nerves. My dad put me on to it when I was a young nigga.

"You a female, and my General. If a nigga put hands on any female that I rock hard with, don't matter if they look like a nigga or a fucking termite, he gon' have to answer to me." I tightened my grip on the steering wheel.

Honor could hold her own; she was as lethal as me when it came to running shit. It's just that niggas had a hard time adjusting and following her direction because she was indeed a female. Honor kept shit organized and she stayed on niggas necks making sure they didn't slack.

"I'm saying it's good because for the past two weeks you been acting unhinged as fuck. I normally call meetings for the gang, so you don't have to waste time, Debo. You can possibly go up in this muthafucka, killing more of our men that we actually need right now." She passed me the blunt that she damn near sucked down. I took it, I needed something potent to get my mind right. I stopped taking percs because I noticed when I was fucking on Praylah, I couldn't bring myself to nut even though I wanted to.

"I ain't that cold." I picked my phone up in the middle console and answered it.

"Alesia, what's good?" I blew smoke from my nose already knowing my assistant was about to give me an ear full.

"Nigga don't what's good me." She spoke low into the phone. "I need you here at the office no later than Friday or I'm coming to find you. There's paperwork that you need to sign off on and the board would like to present some things to you."

It was good owning shit and being a businessman. It was

all the foot work and signing off on shit then sitting in long ass meetings with tight ass suits that got on my fucking nerves.

"Sign off on the shit, Alesia, damn! I got other things that need my attention. Tell the board I'm not open to new ideas or projects right now." I hit the blunt again and pulled into an alley. This nice ass two story house on the Eastside of LA looked like a nice cozy family home from the outside. Niggas from around the way knew it served as headquarters. I had shit built underneath this home that nobody knew about except Ream and Solo and now Honor.

"This is not up for debate, Debo. I handle everything so you won't have to show face as much. Remember this is your company and it requires your time and attention. If you want-"

"Somebody to kiss your ass and do your job... find another slave assistant." I finished her sentence because she loved trying to fake threaten me. "Yea I hear you light bright. I'll see yo' thick ass Friday. Twerk something for a nigga and make it worth my time since you so desperate to see me." She started cursing and yelling, and I hung right up in her face. Alesia's ass stayed having a mini heart attack about my company. That's why I gave her the position, she went above and beyond and kept shit multiplying.

"Remind me to send her crazy ass a flower arrangement today and a spa card. They over there stressing her." I tapped the top of my glove compartment and Honor opened it passing me my nine-millimeter.

"What's up with that nigga Sosa?" I asked before getting out of the car. The sun in Cali was shining hard, I reached back in my Maserati and grabbed my Balenciaga glasses. Opening up the back door, I snatched up my white Balenciaga

shirt and threw that on next. I didn't want any wrinkles in my shit.

"Niggas looking for him." Honor walked around the car and gave me an, 'I told you so look'. I scanned the backyard and frowned at empty bottles of liquor and cups scattered on the grass.

"I told you what the nigga was gon' do. He did good with the first two bricks, gave the nigga four of them birds and now he a week late."

"A week late?" I calmly asked, that made Sosa no longer someone I called a homie. What's crazy is I'd off a nigga for being a day late with my money. Four bricks of yae, was worth his life. Just one brick could put a nigga on, especially after a nigga stepped on it and broke it down. My shit was pure as fuck. I normally sold my shit for twenty-one thousand a brick, but gave Sosa a deal, that was fifteen thousand a brick.

"Yo' veins popping out yo' neck Hulk smash." Honor tried to play it light, but I didn't give a fuck about her dry ass jokes. I bit on my bottom lip to calm myself; I felt like exploding. See, you always need me to guide yo' dumb ass! I told you about this nigga!" Shaking my head to rid myself of that voice, I picked up my size ten foot and kicked the back gate in, knocking it flat on the grass.

"Aye Debo, calm yo' ass down Blood!" Honor was right behind me trying to calm me with words that I ignored.

"Don't tell me to calm down, Honor. Make the call and locate that nigga. I want him found in under an hour." I knocked on the back door and one of my young goons on door duty opened up with an AK in his hands.

"Go clean the front and back fuckin' yard nigga." I marched past him and walked into the front room. As far as I was concerned, I didn't have much time to be here. That's why

I kept my car running so I could do what I had to do and jump right back into my whip and leave.

Entering the room, I chuckled lowly as I eyed every nigga acting frantic when they were just smoking and lounging around. Money was scattered along with empty food containers. I turned around and looked at Honor, her face mirrored mine. Looking at her swollen lip reminded me of why I was here.

I looked over at Dmack and nodded my head at him.

"Honor, why you and this nigga Dmack get into it?" I calmly asked as she stood next to me. I already knew what happened and I believed Honor over all of these niggas. I just wanted to see what his bitch ass had to say.

"Debo, that bitch be tripping. Treating niggas like-" I shook my head no and he stopped talking. See I was a different kind of disrespectful nigga, some would call it ignorance. I lived up to every word that a person had to say 'bout me. Niggas like Dmack was fake and snake as fuck. I had been waiting on a reason to justify my actions by killing this bitch ass nigga.

"See that? How another man can shut you the fuck up right on que? Treating you like the pussy ass nigga you is?" I tilted my head, and he balled his face up.

"What nigga? You ain't a pussy? Cause hitting on some pussy seems real fishy." I chuckled and stepped a little closer to him.

"If you ain't a pussy, stand the fuck up nigga and prove to us that you not a pussy." I removed my gun from my waist and gave it to Honor.

"I respect you too much Debo, I ain't on that my nigga. Honor just be talking to niggas like she some superior ass bitch. Niggas moving weight and working day in and day out. She wanna get mad cause niggas decide to throw a lil get *together the other night." My phone pinged and I checked my message. It was from Soulful, a picture with this nigga Dmack's face right on my screen holding Soulful's wife. Seconds later another text came through with Dmack kissing Soulful's wife lips while she appeared limp.*

I called Soulful right away to get some clarification on the situation.

"I'm standing right in front of the nigga now, what's good baby boy?" I got right to it soon as Soulful answered.

"Ask him how the fuck does he know Jocelyn Hurtz?"

"Jocelyn Hurtz, how the fuck you know her and why was she in your arms passed out? Be real specific." I eyed him not really liking how this shit was gone end up panning out.

"She my lil bitch that be putting me on at the clubs and shit. She be off that yae and I told her to be easy on it. We went out partying, I brought her back here, and we finished the night turning up. She had some yae but claimed she got that shit from the other side, from the getting money niggas." His hands started shaking and he was looking everywhere around the room at his boys like someone was going to save him.

"That shit had fenti in it." Soulful said into the phone.

"We don't do fenti in my product." My jaw clenched because not only was Sosa stomping down hard on the product that I was giving him, he was lacing the bricks with Fentanyl.

"He know where I live, he violated." Soulful added and I nodded my head but said nothing.

"It's handled nigga."

"Bet." He hung up, I turned and took my gun from Honor and aimed it right at Dmack, he tried to duck and move but I was too fast. Two to the dome, brains in his lap. My eyes scanned the room wildly.

"For any of you niggas getting this shit confused and fucked up, let me make this shit clear. Honor is you niggas General. You either honor that or get laid the fuck down. On some real slaughter gang shit, I been nice. Letting niggas breathe and ya baby motha's twerk. Don't ever take my nice, and calmness for some shit you think you will be able to handle. I'm still really like that, the same nigga that make momma's wear all black with big glasses and hats to shield all that mourning they gon' be doing for life."

I eyed every nigga in the room to see which one of these niggas wanted to step up and have some shit to say. Dmack was too mouthy, always trying to appear like he was big and bad when he ain't never put in no major work.

"If you don't like the way the get down is then disappear before I make you disappear. This shit ain't daycare or school. Ain't no bringing hoes to the spot, no partying here, and I bet not ever come around this bitch seeing my shit dirty like this again. The same way you act with me is how you act with Honor." *I nodded my head at Honor, and we walked towards the back to leave.*

"Clean this bitch down and get rid of that nigga." *It wasn't even my intention to kill a nigga today, but Dmack had violated Soulful. If it was my wife and my house, I would want a nigga to act on it if I wasn't able to get to the situation.*

Soon as I got in the car my mind went to Praylah, I wanted to see about her real bad. That shit with Lakendra had fucked me up bad. All these years, I kept taking care of Lakendra because I was under the impression that I was the reason behind her losing our baby. That shit haunted me bad, night and day. Beyond all the bullshit, I really was in love with Lakendra at one point.

She had a lot of selfish ways, but she was the woman that I had fallen for and I overlooked a lot of shit like she did with me. I didn't play her as bad as she thought, I never stuck my dick in a bitch but her when we were together. Lakendra let other hoes get in her head about me when she should have been believing me and what I was telling her.

My father didn't play that shit when it came to honesty. He taught me and all my siblings to stand on everything that came out of our mouths. He couldn't stand a liar; he was always brutally honest and didn't give a fuck who feelings he hurt. I was the same way; I came off as blunt and mean but I always told the truth even when I didn't really want to.

Lakendra lying was the worst thing she could have done besides fucking another nigga in my home. I was a hundred percent sure that she had her foul ass still at my house. I hadn't addressed her or gone around her in two weeks hoping that she saved herself from the embarrassment. To be real, I didn't need any more closure from her, and she didn't need any from me.

All Lakendra needed to do was move the fuck around and get the fuck up out my spot. By now she had enough money and nice things from me from over the years to get on with all her shit.

"So much for you not killing anyone." Honor mumbled under her breath as she started breaking down some weed inside of a hundred-dollar bill.

"Nigga had it coming, he violated with Soulful." I unlocked my phone just as I turned out of the alley and drove around to the front of the house to make sure them niggas was cleaning the front lawn like I had instructed. I didn't want to bring any negative attention to the two-story family home. We didn't have a lot of traffic here, it was a place to count up, cook up, and move shit the fuck out.

I even had my homegirl Tashane living there with her ghetto ass sisters to make that shit believable. Them niggas *throwing a party against my wishes really had me ready to lay them all out but at the same time I understood how shit went. When I was young and getting money, I never followed no niggas orders. I did my own thing and did that shit well. The only difference was, I was a cold devil with my shit.*

I bullied the bullies and the niggas that thought that they could take me on I laid them the fuck out too. The only niggas I never tried to disrespect or overstep was my father and my Uncle Stone. I'd be lying if I said that sometimes both of them niggas made me want to test the waters and get with they asses too. The only thing with that was I knew that my dad was just as nutty as me but fuckin' worse. You tempt the Beast, and all his demons would start spilling out. The only person that could tame him was my mother.

Once I peeped shit out, I chuckled at the frowns plastered on these grown niggas faces as they picked trash up from the front lawn. Going to my messages, I clicked on Praylah's name and went to our thread. I texted and called her one too many times and wasn't feeling how she was curving me. She never came back to the spot that I gave her, and I didn't like that shit.

It had me wondering if she took her ass back to her punk ass baby daddy. I even checked my Beastly Cravings from the website I had set up by Alesia. She had been going to work and from the cameras, she was still driving the car. So, my only question was where the fuck had she been staying. My only answer came back around to her dumb ass being posted back up at the house that she shared with that bitch ass baby daddy of hers.

I didn't give a fuck how mad I got that day, she had to understand that a nigga was just locked deep into my feelings. Finding that bullshit out about Lakendra and how tough she had played me had me thinking all kinds of fucked up things about women in general.

I pulled closer to the curb and got out and walked to the passenger side just as Honor was sealing the blunt. Telling her to drive towards Praylah's old spot, I got comfortable in the passenger seat as I called Praylah's phone blocking my number so she couldn't see that it was me calling.

"No, no, Heaven! Sit down and watch Cocomelon for you get a pop pop!" I listened to Praylah's sexy ass voice, and my heart did some weird shit.

"Umm, hello?" She gave me her attention and for a couple of seconds I didn't know what to say.

"You cheating on me sugar mommy?" I licked my top row of teeth and leaned my seat back, resting my head against the headrest. Sparking up the blunt, I looked over at Honor who was big cheesing and mouthing the words "Simp ass" to me as I flicked her ass off.

"How can I cheat on you when we not even together, Michael?" I could hear the slight attitude in her voice, shit had my dick getting hard. Since I hadn't been taking those damn percs, I was ready to bust a long overdue nut.

"There you go talking all that ditzy ass shit. Fuck I tell you when I slid all inside of that sugar cane?" I smirked at hearing her breathing all hard into the phone. I could just imagine the nervous look that she was sporting on her face. Hitting the facetime option, she accepted. I remained silent as I stared into her pretty ass face. Her cheeks were turning red as she kept blushing and smiling into the phone and a nigga wasn't even saying shit yet.

She had her face so close to the phone that I couldn't see her background. I wasn't tripping though, cause I had the perfect idea of where her ass was at. I was about thirty minutes away from her with gay ass butterflies in my stomach. *This feeling she gave me was some shit that I wanted to feel for forever, so I needed to secure it fast.*

"*That was a bunch of sex talk Michael. We both have too much going on to be trying something serious. I think we need to be friends, get to know each other better and learn each other's triggers.*"

"*I ain't going for that, Praylah. You mine, you hear me sugar?*" *Honor started chuckling, I probably sounded like an old ass man. Honor didn't really need to know the real reasoning behind me calling Praylah sugar.*

"*I'm serious Michael, I still have to figure things out with Heaven's dad. I want a healthy co-parenting relationship with him. I don't want any drama.*" *I pulled at my beard hairs and nodded my head. Praylah didn't know just how deep she was in with me. I'd let her believe whatever bullshit came to her mind about us. I knew what it was and what it wasn't going to be.*

"*Why you over there at that house Praylah?*" *Her eyes grew big as fuck, shit was funny how timid, shy, and scared Praylah was.*

"*I'm gathering some things for Heaven and I. I will now be living with my best friend Era.*" *I got pissed a little but reminded myself that Praylah was trying to be on some fake independent shit since she was done with her bitch ass baby daddy.*

"*Yea alright, I'm fenna fall through. Meet my step-daughter and shit.*" *She shook her head no, fast before she could get the words out. I looked out the window and saw that we were about ten minutes away from her old house.*

"*No, Michael don't do that. I don't want to start anything; Heaven's dad should be home in another hour to visit with her and I know you showing up would just make things uncomfortable.*" *Her voice sounded choppy, and she looked like she was stressed out. I didn't like how this nigga had Praylah so fucking scared. It was time for me to meet and beat the nigga that called himself putting hands on a fucking female.*

"It's time that I meet that nigga anyway. You ain't seen the nigga in a while and I'll be damned if he tries to put his hands on you again. Like I said, I'm on the way." I hung up in her face and put my phone on silent. She was already blowing my phone up and sending texts to stop me from coming. Praylah would learn real fast the way that her man got down.

"You can't bully that girl or her baby daddy, Debo." Honor took the blunt from me and I looked at her with a face that said really?

"I would never bully Praylah but that baby daddy of hers gone get it all. I'm knocking that nigga back just off the strength of him putting his hands on Praylah. If that nigga get too disrespectful then I'm going to body him. Feel me?" We pulled onto Praylah's street.

"No nigga and listen to me now. If you really digging her and want her in the way that you claim, you better be easy on that wanting to kill her baby daddy. No matter how dirty the nigga did her, she still love that nigga and after all its her child's father. You kill him and she might just snitch or better yet really be done with yo' crazy ass." I thought about what Honor said and knew it was true.

I never found myself in a situation like this before, I usually didn't consider other people feelings when it came to killing a nigga. With Praylah I did, I was willing to accept all of her baggage including her daughter. Now the shit had me thinking tough, because Praylah was a square and it was clear that she wasn't used to all the killing and hood shit that

I was on. I was still her boss after all and had to consider that shit too.

Honor pulled up to the curb and I hopped out and tucked my gun in my waist. Checking my surroundings, I strolled up to the porch and tapped on the door twice. Praylah snatched the door open with wide panic-stricken eyes and looked at me in horror. Ignoring all that shit I took a couple of seconds to admire her from head to toe.

Her red hair was curly back in that fro hiding most of her face. She didn't have on any make up, so her face looked a little paler than usual like she hadn't been in the sunlight. Jealously crept over me as I stared at the shape and outline of her curves and the skintight black leggings she had on. Her camel toe looked heavy as fuck sitting upright in her leggings. I eyed the Nikes sports bra and looked up at her like she was crazy.

Praylah pretty ass had too much ass and curves to be dressed the way that she was.

"You tryna get that old thing back or something Pray?" I cocked my head to the side as she shook her head no fast.

"What? No! I told you that I'm moving my things, Michael." I pushed back her mass of curls to see her full face. Pulling her by the chin then kissing her on the cheek on top of that pretty ass colorful birthmark plastered on her cheek, I grabbed a handful of ass and stuck my tongue down her throat.

Giving her a couple of seconds to breathe and look at me with now heavy-lidded eyes, I pecked her again on the lips.

"I'm here to help you move and meet my stepdaughter, sugar mommy. Is that okay with you?" I pushed my hand between her thick thighs and cupped her fat ass pussy.

"Ye- yes Michael that's fine, we just have to be quiet. Ummm Heaven just went down for a nap." She moaned as I cupped her pussy tighter making sure that I applied more pressure.

"Why you telling me all of that? You want me to beat this fat ass pussy up? It's wet for me sugar mommy?" She moaned softly right into my mouth as I licked around her top and bottom lip. I pulled her bottom lip with my teeth and bit down a little with my eyes on hers loving the way they rolled back. She took steps backwards letting me into the house.

I shut the door with my foot not wanting to take my hands off of her soft body.

"I think you make me more fucking crazy in the head Pray. That shit ain't good baby." I picked her up off her feet and walked her towards the room since her baby was on the couch sleep. "I need to feel you, like I gotta bury and print myself deep inside you baby." I licked on her neck; she smelled so fucking good. Once we got in the room I tugged at her legging and made sure to pull her panties down along with her leggings.

"Michael, I haven't taken a shower since early this morning." She covered her pussy like I hadn't already seen it.

"I love your dirty drawls baby. I don't give a fuck if the pussy got a little must to it, that's my pussy, plus it just means that it's been marinating all day for a nigga." She giggled, turning red and shit. Just as I was preparing to pull my dick out of my pants, I heard the sound of a gun clicking behind my head and Praylah screaming at the top of her lungs.

"Jarei please! It's not what you think." I smiled and winked at her, feeling this niggas hot breath on my neck. I turned and was surprised to see this bitch ass nigga that owed me money with a gun to my face.

"Sosa? Oh yea, it's just what you think nigga. Now put that gun down before you hurt yo' self."

DEBO

"*N*ow nigga!" I smirked at Honor that crept up behind this dumb ass nigga. I could feel my jaw ticking because I couldn't believe that this was the nigga who Praylah was getting beat up by. I looked back at Praylah just as I heard Sosa drop the gun and I instantly got pissed with the look that was plastered on her face.

"You still standing there naked? Showing my goods to this nigga? Put some fuckin' clothes on." My anger started to thump throughout my entire body. I was ready to lay this nigga down. The reality was, this was her baby daddy, and I was sure he had seen her naked plenty of times. Now that their shit was over, her body was only for me to see.

"Okay, please don't hurt him." Her pleading for this nigga's life had me tight as fuck and ready to snap at her too. *Kill this nigga! Don't tell me you on some pussy ass shit again.* Shaking my head rapidly, I looked away from Praylah and fixed my eyes on Sosa.

"Where the fuck is my money Sosa? For the sake of yo' baby momma and kid." I don't know what came over me. I knew that I wouldn't harm Praylah nor her daughter, but I felt like she already picked a side and would forever pick this nigga's side since he was right here in the flesh. I wasn't about to be the nigga being in competition with the next nigga over pussy.

"I got yo' money my nigga, why is you here bout to fuck my bitch." He gritted. I chuckled and cracked my neck from side to side.

"Step outside Sosa. If my bread not in your car, then go in that living room and kiss ya daughter goodbye. I would tell you to kiss ya bm too but that's my bitch. She just being a stupid bitch for you right now. When she should be begging me to kill you for knocking her grill out." I looked back and offered Pray's funky ass an icy look. She had me so pissed that I didn't want to see her face right now. Had me battling with my mental ready to snap, I was struggling with keeping my composure since she was right here and her daughter in the other room. If she wasn't here right now, I wouldn't even be giving this nigga Sosa a chance. His brains would have been decorated the carpet.

"I got yo bread my nigga, I just needed more time. This dike ass bitch been riding my dick hard about the money I was planning on bringing you personally. I wanted to triple up the next time that I re'd up and knew she would start talking all that tough shit, so I was trying to meet with you." He spat as I could see the fire in Honor's eyes. I knew the nigga was lying because if that was the case then Sosa would have called me and asked to meet. Who the fuck did this nigga think I was? *A straight pussy that's who! Now prove him wrong!*

"Is that right?" I smirked and nodded my head, just as Sosa began to open his mouth, Honor knocked him over the top of his head with the butt of her gun causing him to fall down hard with a loud thud. I couldn't help but chuckle at the piss stain that became evident on his pants as he snored loudly with his mouth open.

"What the hell! Oh my, look you have to go! Right now, Michael!" I looked over at Praylah and decided to get into her personal space. Marching over to where she stood, I tried my hardest to ignore her wide-ass hips and thick luscious thighs. Getting pissed all over again that this nigga Sosa interrupted me from busting a big ass nut. I moved all in Praylah's face and her timid ass moved backward until her back hit the wall in her bedroom.

"You don't listen well." I placed my hand above her head, not moved by her bottom lip trembling. "That nigga that you call your baby daddy laid out taking a nap right now owes me lots of fucking money. You over here panicking and shit and begging for this nigga's safety making me look crazy in front of my homie Honor. I can't respect a woman who refuses to respect herself Pray. This nigga done beat you, knocked ya teeth out and only God, you, and him know what else he has done to you." I thought back to the day that I finally broke her ass down and got between her legs and looked at her like she was fucking insane.

"You should let me meet your daughter real soon, I'm her dad now. I'm about to call my momma, give her this address so she can come talk to you. I think she can help you understand me better. Go shower and get dressed."

"You don't remember all the shit I told you about my mental. How that voice inside of my head done fell in love with you? How I told you that I'd kill to keep you, Praylah... you can't play that ditzy dumb shit with me, baby. I ain't all there in the fuckin' head. See, I know that shit already, but I don't give a fuck. Put on some fuckin' clothes before I fuck you right here in front of ya bitch ass baby daddy that's knocked out cold in front of everybody." Her bottom lip trembled and the sane part of me told me to cool it.

I even tried to count down in my head several times like my father instructed me to do whenever that voice started raging loud and wild inside of my head, but nothing seemed to work.

"See this the foul shit Lakendra did to me. Bitch played with my fucking head had me wishing that I put her ass in a ditch somewhere. Now you standing in front of me acting all scared and shit like I wasn't just cleaning yo' ass and promising you some shit that I wouldn't dare take back. I might be crazy or whatever muthafuckas try to say I am but one thing about me is, I'm a real ass nigga." The back of my neck started to throb, and I could feel a migraine coming on because of me being so angry and unable to focus on one subject at a time.

I had Praylah in front of me, her face was red, and fear was evident, and she still hadn't put on her fucking clothes like I instructed her to do. Then I had this bitch ass nigga Sosa, who was my so-called homie. I fucked with him on a real street level and showed the nigga some love. Only for him to be a week late with my payment.

I knew that if I killed him right now, Praylah would only be more petrified and find a way to get away from me. Then again, I was a nigga that had made a solid foundation and didn't like my rules being bent or broken. I had to reason and that voice inside of my head only wanted blood on my hands right now which was making shit even more complex. On top of that I didn't show the fact that Sosa being Praylah's baby daddy surprised the fuck out of me.

It should've turned me away from her, but it was too late. That voice and myself wanted Praylah's timid ass bad and I didn't know exactly why. From the first time I laid eyes on her red ass, I knew I wanted her. I probably would have still wanted her even if I knew she was Sosa's.

"I am scared, I have to push my fear to the side to think about Heaven. She is my everything and I cannot and will not lay down with a man that harms her father." She couldn't even look me in the eyes as she was talking, which infuriated me even more.

"So, you telling me that you are willing to lay down with a nigga that beats you and not get you the help that you need? You want your daughter to grow up thinking that its cool for her nigga to beat her too?" I shook my head and looked deep into her pretty big eyes.

"You picking this nigga over me, Praylah? You don't want me?" I looked over at Honor and she gave me a sad look that had me swallowing down my pride. She'd never even seen me this way with Lakendra, so I knew this shit was different for her. I was happy that it was Honor that was here with me than any of my other soldiers. This was a weak ass moment for me, and I probably would never forgive myself for even begging Praylah with my eyes for her not to say the wrong fucking thing.

"I'm picking my daughter, Michael. Jarei is her father, I don't want any more drama." Tears fell down her face and I grabbed her softly by the bottom of her chin. I was surrounded by heat and fiery, but I didn't want to kick her when she was obviously conflicted and confused. Later she would see that she'd made a grave mistake. I grabbed each ass cheek and pulled her close to me. Bending down to connect with her soft plump lips I pecked her twice, then turned away from her.

That shit had me feeling fucked up on some weird shit, but I wouldn't dare make myself look crazier.

"Stay safe and love yourself more, Pray." I walked away from her even though I didn't want to.

"Go check that nigga car for all of my money plus more," I ordered Honor as she turned and walked out the room. Looking down at Sosa and then back at Praylah, I shook my head at her. I couldn't believe she was about to pass up an opportunity with me. I wouldn't have wanted shit in return from her but loyalty. A street nigga like myself needed calm and peace to come home to. It wasn't on some conventional normal type of shit, but what could possibly be normal for a nigga like me? I had more money than I needed and had the respect and street credit to go along with it.

I owned my own franchises and made money with my eyes closed. I could have any bitch I wanted but I wanted a female that could make me feel like none of that shit mattered. Looking down at Sosa he was slowly waking up. I picked my foot up and stomped him right in his face and knocked his bitch ass back out.

"Get out!" Praylah yelled and I ignored her ass and kept walking out. She just didn't understand how she was really a saving grace for this nigga right now. When I made my way outside, Honor was already loading my car with duffle bags of what I was sure was money and probably drugs. Honor was as cold as it got. If I told her to go strip a muthafucka down, she would do just that and take every single thing else a person had attached to them.

I jumped in the car and lit a blunt immediately to try to cool my nerves. Praylah's face kept popping up into my mental making it hard for me to concentrate.

"Everything there plus some new work that the nigga tried to get from some other niggas." She pulled off slowly from Praylah's block as I remained quiet not really knowing what to say.

"What you want me to do about that nigga? I can have some niggas run down on him tonight." I shook my head no, and looked over at her as I released the smoke from my mouth.

"Let the nigga live for now. Praylah too green when it comes to that nigga." I spat, disgusted with what I was even saying. If I wanted a nigga dead or even had a simple thought of offing a nigga, it happened and here I was for the sake of Praylah's ditzy ass telling Honor to let this bitch ass nigga live. Niggas that violated usually got the worse treatment from me. If you violated me, I felt like it was only right for me to violate you even worse. Honor always said I went overboard with punishment. The voice in my head always said that I didn't even do enough.

"She will come around big dog. Just gotta let her be and figure her shit out. She got to want better for herself. Don't get caught up in that until she's serious about you too." Honor placed her hand on my shoulder, and I felt every word she was spitting. The only problem was my need for getting or having whatever it was that I wanted. Praylah, I wanted her like I wanted power over the streets. I needed her like I needed air to breathe. I hoped she didn't think this shit was over like I was some pussy ass nigga.

The only reason I gave her delicate ass a pass today was because of her beautiful daughter laying in that living room sound asleep. I didn't want my stepdaughter to meet me for the first time and think that I was some sort of monster. I only wanted Heaven to have good times and look up to a nigga. Fuck what Praylah was talking about and fuck her for the time being.

ERA

"Get this nigga in the chair and tell him to see about me!" I looked on with wide eyes at all three of my triplet uncles, they were at each other's throats. While it was entertaining it all got taken to a whole other level and now Uncle Lenny, who was paralyzed from the waist down, wanted to fight from his wheelchair over a prostitute that Uncle Denny took from him.

Anytime Uncle Lenny felt like one of his brothers had disrespected him, he would demand for them to sit in a chair so he could fight them from his wheelchair. I sipped on my Stella Rose as I watched from behind my mom's kitchen island at my uncles going at it over a hoe that had to be something big with the way Uncle Lenny and Denny were at each other's throats.

"The bitch is my hoe! Both of you niggas owe me money. The pussy that I serve ain't cheap and my prices is steep. Both of you nigga's can fight but I want my doe ray meh around this muthafucka, understand?" Uncle Benny popped his collar and threw his hand behind his back. I stifled a laugh because he was always super smooth with his words. He instigated the most when it came to his brothers but never ended up being the one fighting. He was something else and always claimed that he was too purty to have a hair on his head misplaced.

Uncle Denny and Lenny wore their hair in short-tapered curls, they had salt and pepper colored hair while Uncle Benny had my mom dye his hair black every first of the month. His hair was always pressed going past his broad shoulders with a long beard that he made my momma press as well. The triplets were identical, but you could easily tell Uncle Benny apart from Lenny and Denny.

"I got your money, but I told this nigga not to sleep with Essence! She's mine!" Uncle Lenny pounded his chest, and I couldn't believe that he was this serious over a prostitute.

"You one crazy nigga. The hoe is mine, she married to the game Lenny. See, I done told you about paying for pussy. Especially the type of pussy I provide, Essence is a hoe of mine that will never walk away even if I gave her my famous walking papers. You know the papers when a hoe has too many miles on the pussy and the tricks don't want it anymore. Why get mad if Denny pays to lay with her? You know how many niggas lay with her in a day?" Uncle Benny's voice was calm but I could now hear the frustration in his voice.

He hated breaking my uncles up whenever they fought but he always seemed entertained by the drama and the arguments they presented.

"I don't give a fuck. Sit in that chair and come see about me nigga!" Uncle Lenny roared and Uncle Benny shook his head in defeat. He went and got a folding chair and sat it right in front of Uncle Lenny. Uncle Denny cracked his knuckles and gave Uncle Lenny a mean glare.

"I ain't taking shit easy just cause you in that wheelchair

nigga. I'm knocking your ass right out that muthafucka. When I'm done, I'll pay this nigga Benny two thousand more dollars to fuck that pretty thang again!" Uncle Lenny couldn't wait for Uncle Denny to get in the chair. His hands shook from anger as he rolled towards Uncle Denny and rolled his feet over causing him to yelp and scream out in pain.

"You stay away from her!" Uncle Lenny reversed and rolled over Uncle Denny feet again just as Uncle Denny limped his way in the chair. I could tell Uncle Denny was in pain, but he was trying his hardest not to show it. Both men got close until they were knee to knee and started fighting. Blow for blow they weren't letting up on each other until Uncle Lenny's arms got tired from swinging on Uncle Denny. Uncle Denny got the best of Uncle Lenny and knocked him back causing his wheelchair to roll backward into my mom's glass crystal dove vase. They hoisted her flowers that some mystery man brought her every Sunday when she came from church.

I was still trying to figure out who the nigga was, but my mom was very sneaky and secretive thanks to her having three brothers that tried to stay in her business.

"Earlene beating all of our asses." Uncle Benny shook his head and tried to pick the glass pieces from the vase up, but it was too late. My mom stood in the hallway with her curlers still in her head. She had the house phone glued to her ear with her shoulder holding it up. A lit blunt dangled from her thin lips as she blinked several times. Something she did whenever she was angry. She kept batting those false long curly lashes as if she was in some type of dream and her vase being broken was not real.

"Shirley, I'm fenna fuck some niggas up, bless they soul. I have to call you back." I assumed that she didn't give her friend Shirley time to say bye because she had already tossed her cordless phone onto her leather sectional couch and stomped from the hallway to the utility closet that was in the kitchen. She mumbled stuff the whole time, you could hear her rambling through the closet.

"My momma gave me that vase! I don't know why these niggas like to lay up and chose they fights at my damn house. Oh, but they gone learn today! In Jesus name! They gone learn today!" She talked loud enough for all of us to hear. I looked at my uncle's faces and felt a little sorry for them. They all had scary looks on their faces as Uncle Benny was already tucking his tail, smoothing his hair down he picked up his hat that had a white feather leaning on the left side and tried to smoothly walk out.

He was too late on leaving because my mom flew in the room like a bat straight from hell and went after him first. You know how a kid get they ass beat by their mom? The whole time a momma beats her kid's ass she explains why she's beating their asses. That's what my mom was doing to my uncle's right at this very moment with a broomstick. Every hit was connecting, and I cringed at every hit that landed. I could almost feel the sting and cringed while my mom huffed and puffed beating ass.

"Come on now Earlene! You gon' make me sweat this fresh press out! I didn't do anything." Instead of my Uncle Benny covering his body or even his face, he kept checking his hair by running his hands through it. I giggled when he shook his head from side to side to make sure his silk press was still giving body and moving with each twist and turn of his neck.

"Get yo' fake pimping limping ass out Benny! Lenny roll bounce ya ass up out of here and Denny you better follow 'fore I get my deuce and start shooting!" My mom struggled to catch her breath but turned and walked out of the room.

My uncles groaned and rubbed at the places that were obviously hurting them.

"Era come help ya uncle out." Uncle Lenny asked. I opened the door and rolled him right out of the house. Saying my goodbyes, I decided to give my mom some space. We all had been crowding her space for the past couple of weeks. I didn't like being at home by myself and lost in my thoughts, so I practically stayed over here where it was convenient. I got to laugh and feel loved because my mom and uncles were close. It wasn't a day that passed by that you didn't see or hear of them together.

Walking down the long hallway that led to my mom's room, I could hear her sniffling. She looked up at me and wiped at her tears. My mom was angry and hurt and I knew it had to do with her vase.

"My mom gave me that! Them fools know how much I love that vase. Now they done broke it." I sat next to her and pulled her in for a hug.

"I'm sorry ma, you want me to cook for you before I leave?" She slowly pulled out of my embrace and wiped her face then cleared her throat. I had never seen someone transform that fast from crying to being absolutely fine.

"No, I'm fine, I have a date and I need to be getting ready for that." I looked at her shocked because she sure was going out a little more than normal.

"Who is this guy ma?" I gave her a curious look and she just blushed and touched the curling rods in her hair to make sure they were still in place.

"He's just a friend chile. How's Praylah doing? I tried calling her and she didn't answer." She changed the topic fast and I caught on to her not wanting to tell her business to me, yet she loved knowing all of me, including Praylah.

"I don't know, I have to go see about her but don't want

to run into that man of hers." I shook my head. Praylah was back with Jarei and I didn't know why. She didn't explain it much, but she said she felt like it was best to work on her family no matter how imperfect it was. I hated that for her, but she had to find her own backbone. I was starting to become used to Praylah's indecisive mind. One moment she was done then the next she was doing it for Heaven. Which was a weak ass excuse.

"I wish she could let him go; I'll be praying hard for her. That boy is the devil." My mom picked up her phone, the screen lit up, and she smiled like she saw a message that had her super geeked.

"Your father called, said he wanted to meet with you sometime next week." My stomach instantly dropped. I didn't like the fact that my father always called my mom first as if I was a kid when it came time to see or even talk to me. I knew that he really didn't even want to see about me. He just liked to somehow have an excuse to talk to my mom.

"Why didn't he just call me and say that instead of making it weird."

"Chile, I don't know. I wish the nigga would just call you. Every time I hear his voice, I run to the bathroom to take a shit because he makes my stomach hurt that bad." Silence fell over us and we both fell out laughing. My mom couldn't stand my father and she had every right to feel how she felt. My dad didn't really want to see me like I said. Usually if he did, he would send one of his famous long text that he sent every other year when he was feeling guilty of not being a good father. I loved him still, but he was sorry as hell in the dad department. Now that I was grown it didn't bother me much. I just was over getting worked up and hopeful with him.

I stayed and talked a little longer with my mom then

finally said my goodbyes. I made my way to my car and headed straight home. I guess I would finish enjoying my day off since it was right back to work for me tomorrow. I still didn't know if Praylah would show face at work. I hope she did because the last thing her ass needed to do was quit and become dependent on her nothing-ass baby daddy.

Pulling in front of my house my phone started ringing on cue. I frowned at the unknown number but still answered out of curiosity.

"Hello?" I placed the phone on speaker.

"Hello, am I speaking with Era?" The voice belonged to a woman. Her voice was soft and low.

"Yes, this is her, may I ask who is calling?"

"Sure, this is Shelby Watts. I'm a friend of Soulful Hurtz. I wanted to set a time and date to sit down and meet with you. Soulful sent me a couple of videos of you from Instagram and you have talent and the voice to go along with it." Her voice cheered up and my stomach fluttered for multiple reasons.

Soulful Hurtz was still on my mind heavy when he shouldn't have been. The man was fine and knew exactly what to do with all the dick he was packing. Too bad he was another cheating dog that happened to be married. I wouldn't let that mess up the great connection he gave me with Shelby.

"I've been blackballed by my ex-boyfriend Devin. He produces and also manages big celebrities; the list goes on of all the things he contributes to the industry. I caught him cheating and broke up with him. He promised me that I wouldn't get far. So, I'm letting you know this because I don't want to waste your time." I blurted that out fast. My mom always taught me to keep it real and be upfront. She taught me that time meant everything, and to demand for people to respect my time and that I should respect theirs.

"I've had a few clients that were supposed to be blackballed but now they're multimillionaires. I don't want you worrying who this so-called pig of an ex is. You give me his name and trust me when I say my connects and reach will triumph right over him." I smiled at that because since my encounter with Devin and him showing me that contract, I felt super helpless. It felt like I would never reach my biggest dreams.

I loved to cook but I was in love with singing. It did something to me every single time I hit a high or low note. Singing repaired all of the hurt I ever endured. It was therapy for my soul and mind, so I never planned on stopping. I just thought that I would never get far.

"His name is Devin." Shelby would be the first person that I admitted this too. I didn't want to tell my mom or uncles because I knew that if I told them how dirty Devin was playing with me, they wouldn't hesitate to touch him.

"He will not be a problem. Now tell me Era, are you ready to become a big star? Because that's where you will be headed working with me. There will be late nights, early mornings, and things will move fast as hell. I can promise you, with your voice and my expertise, we will go far. All you have to do is give me a day and time to meet and I will send you the address to my office." My eyes welled up with tears, I could hear my heart beating through my eardrums.

"Tomorrow. I can meet with you tomorrow, anytime." This was big and I was hopeful that Mr. Brownston would understand me calling off of work. Before I called him, I planned on calling Praylah to see if she could cover for me so I wouldn't have to bother Mr. Brownston.

"Great, I was hoping you said tomorrow. I will send you the time and address. See you tomorrow, Era."

"Thank you, see you tomorrow." I hung the phone up and just stared at it for a couple of seconds not believing the call I just got. If I had Soulful's number, I would call him and thank him a million times but then again, I didn't want to bother. The man was married and probably didn't want to be reached. My disappointment in Soulful almost took over me until I pushed it away. I already made myself accept that he was a married man, and I had no business even thinking about him.

That was a hard task when he blessed me big time by sending Shelby my way. It also made me wonder how he even got my number to give to Shelby when we never exchanged digits. Then again, men like Soulful could do just about anything he wanted to with the money he had.

I checked out my house and noticed a couple of kids on bikes riding by. My neighborhood was peaceful way quieter than where my mom stayed at in south-central LA. Focusing back on my phone, I called Praylah first. It rang a couple times then went straight to voicemail. Getting pissed off with her ignoring me and me having to cover for her at work, I called again. I couldn't keep covering and hiding the fact that she hadn't come in to work for over two weeks. Mr. Brownston was a businessman, he wouldn't hesitate to fire her ass no matter how much he liked her he was a firm believer in setting a perfect example and he never showed favoritism. His favorite saying was, "a job is a job".

"Damn bitch, why the fuck you keep calling?" I could hear Heaven whining in the background and that pulled at my heartstrings tough.

"Nigga who the fuck you calling, bitch?" I looked at the phone like I was daring Jarei to confess who he was talking so boldly to.

"You bitch! My bitch can't be friends with yo' burnt skillet fat ass. Stop texting her about that fuck ass job and asking if she is okay. Praylah ain't working that job nor coming around yo' ugly fat ass no more. She a stay-at-home mother now." He chuckled at the last part and I wish me and him were face-to-face so I could stomp his damn private parts out.

"Look how insecure and controlling you sound. You know your little small-time hustling ass can't keep a solid income coming but now your ego is bruised. I can't wait until Praylah sees how she doesn't need your needy ass! She has her parents and me to help and back her. Oh, and not only does she have us, she has Debo, nigga! So, if something happens to her, you might as well kiss your pathetic ass life away!" I hung up before he could say anything. I said a quick silent prayer for my best friend hoping that she would snap out of whatever trance she was in.

I knew all about my boss Mr. Brownston and heard stories around South Central and other parts of Los Angeles about the infamous Debo. He was a street rich nigga and anybody that spoke of him, had fear in their voices from the things he had done. I kept things respectful all the time and referred to him as Mr. Brownston, because when it came to him taking care of business, he was nothing but respectful and professional. I didn't see the side that everyone talked about around the way. Staring into his cold, stone eyes I could tell that the nigga had a dark side.

It was only a matter of time before I would have to ask for his help when it came to Praylah. I wasn't going to run away from her or fear for my life just because Jarei was trying to place her on lock down. In a couple of days, Ju'well and my mom along with her baby, deuce deuce, and I would pay Praylah a visit and see just how tough Jarei would act face-to-face. Jarei wasn't shit but a fucking coward.

I went ahead and called Debo to let him know that I had to call off. I was sure he would have his assistant Alesia reach out to a manager from one of his other restaurants to have them step in for me. Mr. Brownston was serious about his identity not being exposed. He loved to see how his restaurants were running without people faking and acting like they were doing their job just because he came around.

"What's up Era?" His deep voice came through the line, and I could tell that something was bothering him.

"Hey, Mr-" I started but was cut off abruptly.

"You like family now since you best friends with my girl. So, call me Debo, never call me Michael, that's for Praylah." He sounded so serious that I had to stifle my laugh so he wouldn't feel disrespected. In his mind, Praylah was his and I couldn't be mad at a determined man.

"Okay, Debo." I smiled and then continued. "I need someone to cover me, I have a meeting with a potential new manager for my music career. I just don't want to miss this opportunity."

"I feel you and I hope it works out for you... Drag that nigga to the fuckin' back!" my eyes got big as I checked my surroundings. I could hear Debo's background and it sounded really busy. His voice got deep and dark, shit, he sounded scary.

"My bad Era, look I'm in the middle of some business shit, call Pray and tell her to cover you. I notice she been missing too many days anyway." I swallowed hard because I never reported that. He chuckled like he knew that I was shocked by him revealing that.

"Trust, Era... I know everything when it comes down to my business. You good though, I respect your loyalty to your friend. Make sure you tell her to get her ass to work or I'm firing her pretty ass. Family and girlfriends don't exclude me from terminating someone from my payroll." He stated seriously and I shook my head because I hated to deliver the bad news. I had been trying my hardest to make sure she kept her job but with the way Jarei sounded it seemed as if that was done for.

"Debo, I called her and Jarei answered. He is so ignorant, and I don't think he is allowing her to work anymore given the circumstances." The line went quiet, even his background. I could hear his deep breaths come through on the phone which indicated that he was still on the call with me.

"So, you haven't heard from her at all?" He quizzed in a worried tone.

"No, I haven't." I sighed, feeling defeated.

"Bet. I'll call my assistant and have her send someone in your place tomorrow. I'll pay Praylah a visit." I smiled at that.

"Thanks, Debo."

"Say less." He hung up and I started gathering my things feeling happy that my best friend had someone like Debo to look after her.

PRAYLAH

My brain felt so heavy with overwhelming thoughts that whenever I tried to sit up to get out of bed, my head pounded hard. I couldn't think straight to save my life, but I was happy that Heaven wasn't here with me to witness me this way. Jr. was here though and at this point, I didn't have the strength to really tend to him. He laid next to me and rubbed his tiny hands through my hair, I found that to be soothing and comforting.

Nyla dropped baby Jarei off this morning, and I woke up to him in bed with me. The icing on the cake and what really drained the color from my once vibrant apricot skin tone was that Nyla got evicted and was now living under the same roof as me and Jarei. Jarei treated Nyla like she was delicate. He didn't yell or call her names. He almost acted as if he was scared of her. The both of them came in and out as they pleased, leaving me here to tend to the house but lately, I haven't even been doing that.

It's been two weeks, and I could count the number of days that I attempted to do anything worthwhile. When Heaven was here, I took my medicine and smiled at all the insults that were being hurled my way just to keep the peace. It was a big relief when my mom and dad came up to get Heaven. Whenever Heaven went away, I was able to slip into my heavy depression in peace and not feel so guilty about the dangerous thoughts I had inside my mind.

When Michael stood in front of Jarei, I could feel the anger radiating off of him onto me. I had to check myself when I had thoughts of telling Michael to actually kill him when Jarei walked in on me and Michael getting ready to have sex. With Michael, I felt a comfort that I never felt in a man before. I felt secure and safe, like I could trust him with my life. The main thing that scared me was how attached we seemed to be in such a short period of time.

Now here I was feeling back low and so weak that I was disgusted with my own existence. I had been low before, but this was a different type of low. I felt like a prisoner of all my negative thoughts and feelings. I was so indecisive and couldn't seem to sort my shit out. That in itself was very frustrating. Going on a rollercoaster feeling like I had advanced a little bit but got set back majorly and ended up landing back to square one. In this hell hole of a house with people that didn't give two fucks about me. What made it worse was that I barely cared about myself.

I was praying for my sanity, but I felt myself losing my grip. I couldn't stop thinking about Michael and after I turned him away the way that I did trying to defend Jarei, I knew that he wouldn't come around. I didn't even want to show my face to him and see the look of disappointment. I appreciated him trying to help me but that scared me too. I never had anyone outside of my parents, Era, and Ju'well do something nice for me without wanting something in return. That was just my sad truth.

"Girl, that's why he treats you like that. Get yo' ass in the shower and do ya hair or something." I sat up a little from my tear-stained pillow and looked over at the door at Nyla. She looked beautiful like a model, and I wished I could be her size and look like her just to see how it felt to be treated good; to be waited on and to have whatever I practically wanted. I hated how my thinking process worked. How much I doubted myself then I'd turn around on good days and have all the confidence in the world. How ironic, half the time I didn't want to be me. I lacked so much as a woman and wanted to desperately do better so my daughter wouldn't eventually catch on and think this shit was cool.

"I don't want him to touch me." I mumbled and decided to sit all the way up in bed and ignore the pounding on the left side of my head.

"Then why the fuck you here Pray?" She leaned against the door just as Jr. planted a kiss on my cheek making me smile lazily at him. He got off the bed and went right up to his mom. No matter how distant Nyla was with her son, he loved and adored his mother just how Heaven was with me.

"I did it for Jarei's safety, I didn't want him getting killed and leaving our kids without a dad. I do love Jarei. I'm just not in love with him anymore and I can't sort out why I'm so weak and still here." I shrugged, not even caring how embarrassing my truth sounded.

"You hear cause if you leave me again bitch, I'm taking Heaven. You're not fit to keep her on your own. You and I both know that shit." Jarei spat standing so close behind Nyla that his dick was touching her ass. I knew they were fucking right under my nose, but I didn't give a damn about that either.

"Why though Jarei?" I stood off the bed as Nyla and Jarei both looked at me with utter disgust. "I'm fat, funky, all I'm good for is cooking from time to time and watching the kids.

Why not let me be? At least I'm a good mother to our daughter and your son? You cheat on me all the time, I only cheated once and that was because I never got treated the way Michael…" Before I could finish Jarei was across the room standing right in front of me.

He grabbed me up by the throat and squeezed so tight I thought he might snap my neck. Dragging me to the bathroom he pushed me onto the toilet seat. Starting the bath water, he ran hot water, I watched trying to see if he was going to add cold water, but he never did. I started tapping my left leg, growing nervous. I didn't know what he was getting ready to do and fear ran all through my bones. He snatched up a bottle of my bath and body works soap and squeezed almost the whole bottle into the tub.

"Laying around here crying and worrying about the next nigga in my house. Bitch got me fucked up!" He mumbled all kinds of things under his breath as hot tears fell down my face.

"Just let me go live with my parents or Era. Let me just be the nothing-ass bitch that I truly am Jarei. I promise to take care of Heaven but being here with you is killing me!" I yelled frustrated with myself and Jarei.

"Well then die bitch!" He gritted, staring at me with hate.

"I won't die as long as my daughter is alive. She is my reason." I argued.

"Well, then bitch get comfortable cause you ain't going nowhere! You my bitch! You think cause my homie Debo mental ass took a liking to you that you gone run off and be happy with that nigga? Like I'ma actually let you go be with him and have more money than me when bitch I been grinding to feed and pay bills for you and Heaven!"

"I pay bills Jarei! You never-"

Whap!

23

I felt dazed as he closed fist hit me. I felt myself hitting the tiled floor until he grabbed me by my matted down fro and tossed me in the scorching hot tub like I weighed nothing. The water burnt me so bad that it felt like I passed out momentarily. The tub overflowed as he pushed my head under. Nose burning, water filling me up, I couldn't breathe, and I panicked. He brought my head up and I choked and threw up trying to catch my breath as I clutched onto his forearm for dear life.

"Ja... reiiii pleaseeee!" I choked and begged. "I'll do better please!" I cried but accepted my fate and welcomed it. I said a silent prayer for my daughter hoping that she would forgive me. Maybe this was meant to be. Looking in Jarei's eyes I knew that it was a wrap for me. He pushed my head back under and I didn't even attempt to breathe or struggle against him anymore.

"What the fuck nigga, is you insane!" I heard Nyla and the next thing I knew I felt like I was floating on water watching Nyla swing and hit on Jarei to save me. I wished she didn't do that, but I guess I should be grateful.

"Mind your business, Nyla! This between me and my bitch!" Jarei yelled. My body felt numb, and I couldn't move but I saw the steam rising from my body and water.

"Nigga I'm not fenna let you just kill her! No matter what you say she does do a lot for us!" She turned the hot running water off and carefully stepped closer then reached toward the cold-water knob and turned it on. I couldn't feel shit because my body was blazing and numb if that made any sense.

Nyla looked into my eyes and dropped tears of her own. I was all cried out, if I made it out of this, I would never come back to Jarei. I just needed my phone to get away. Jarei didn't know that him trying to kill me and me almost accepting that fate was a reality check to myself.

"Jarei get out before I call my brothers and have them fuck you up." Nyla threatened. Surprisingly he listened and walked away looking at me like he was disgusted and pissed that he couldn't do what he was really trying to do.

"Come on girl, let me help you." Nyla gathered all her long weave up and rolled it around until it was balled up into a bun on top of her head. My body felt like it was scalded and burnt all over. Looking down at my skin it was the color red. My body trembled and I think I was in so much shock and pain that my cry was trapped into my throat. Holding Nyla's hand as I stepped out, trying my hardest to steady my steps so I wouldn't fall on the wet floor, I heard the front door slam.

"I didn't do anything Nyla. All I did was love him. It's hard for me to control when I slip into a bipolar episode or get depressed, but I have been good to him through it all." My tears were finally falling but I couldn't feel them.

"That's no excuse and you gotta stand up for yourself. You got the right to talk and say how you feel as an adult. Don't ever let a nigga take that from you. Not even me. I apologize to you as well I just didn't like you cause it felt like you took my man from me when in reality I never had no business fooling with Jarei's broke ass." She looked off then wiped at her tears before they fell and ruined her makeup.

"I'm moving to Atlanta with my parents until I get on my feet. It's some balling ass niggas up there that will sweep me off my feet with my son. I ain't looking back cause Jarei don't give a damn about these kids. You should do the same. Love don't pay the fucking bills Praylah." We walked into the room that Jarei and I shared. I sat on the bed while she moved around the room freely like she was well acquainted with where everything was. She brought me some sweats and a top with some mango Shea butter.

"Rub that all over so your body won't scab from that hot ass water." I did as she instructed.

"Jarei just mad cause he doesn't understand why a paid nigga like Debo wants you. Shit, I ain't understand it either." She chuckled and rolled her eyes.

"I was just being jealous. I need a nigga like Debo, shit would have me set for life. Girl, you need to get Heaven and disappear, go with Debo, Jarei not gon' do shit to you if you with him trust. That nigga Debo got his bitch ass spooked like my brothers got him spooked."

"I don't want nothing from Michael, I just want to work on myself for Heaven." Nyla smacked her lips.

"That's cool and all, see women like you is what niggas pray for Praylah. You're humble and pretty, very smart and you not a selfish bitch like me. Listen to me and listen clear baby girl... if you stay here, that nigga Jarei gon' end up killing you. He ain't happy with himself, he still a struggling ass hustler tryna figure some shit out. He gon' project all that shit on you. Hell, my momma bipolar and she get depressed too. It's all about who you around, with your mental shit. Being around Jarei just gon' make the shit worse. Hurry up and get dressed so you can leave while you got the chance girl. I'm only helping you this one time, baby momma number two." She smirked and I tried to smile back but my face felt tight from the hot water.

I stood up and put on my clothes not caring to put deodorant on or fix my hair. I felt like time was ticking and I did want to be gone by the time Jarei came back.

Getting me and Heaven's social security cards and all my important information together and stuffing it in my purse, I headed for the front door passing Nyla up. Nyla had her feet kicked up on the coffee table smoking a blunt.

"Thank you, Ny." I looked at her, still surprised that she saved me.

"You welcome girl, now gone." She winked at me. My hand shook as I reached for the doorknob thinking that I was going to run into Jarei. I didn't have a phone or any money and didn't know how I would make it to my parents' house or even Era's but like Nyla stated, I needed to get away.

As soon as I opened the door, it felt like I ran into a tall tree that smelled good.

"You ready to come home?" My eyes traveled up to Michael's gray eyes that were set dead on me. He stood so tall and looked so fine that my mouth watered at the sight of him. This man was really like my guardian angel. A calm came over me and I felt all the anxiety leave my body as I slowly nodded my head. He looked me over like he was inspecting me, and I didn't care, I just wanted him to take me far away from here.

"He- he tried... to..." My shoulders slumped down, and I found myself not being able to find the words needed to communicate what just happened with Jarei and I. I was still stuck on the fact that he really tried to drown me. Michael's dreads were freshly twisted going back into a ponytail. He smelled so good and looked even better. With a white Polo shirt on and dark blue denim jeans, he had on some all-white Air Force Ones that looked fresh out the shoe box.

I don't know what made him come here but I was forever grateful once again for his presence.

"Let's go, we will talk about it when we get home." I nodded my head and grabbed his hand and let him lead me right to his all-black Cadillac Escalade.

When we got inside of his car Jarei was speeding into the

driveway. He hopped out of his car just as Michael grabbed his gun. My heart start beating fast in my chest, I couldn't make out what Jarei was saying. Michael's eyes turned dark, he looked over at me and stared deep into my eyes as Jarei yelled and tapped hard on the window. This time I could hear him telling me to get out of the car.

"Sugar mommy, listen to me. Focus only on me for a second baby." He was talking to me calmly but his jaws were clenched.

"I don't want shit from you, not even pussy if you don't want to give that up. That shit good as fuck but I'm willing to wait for it. I don't want to rush you in no form of commitment, but I know I'd act a fucking donkey on any nigga that's trying to get close to you. I'm really digging the fuck out of you, and I know one day, I'll be able to explain better on why I feel so captivated and attached to you." He grabbed my hands and enclosed them with his. Totally ignoring Jarei, he leaned forward over the car console and kissed me passionately, stealing my breath away.

"That nigga out there is dead, I ain't gon' kill him yet cause I want him to prove to you why his mere existence isn't needed. I'm a stone-cold killer baby. I make niggas like him go away for less. He don't love you, he love the control he has over you. He like to see you weak as fuck and second guessing yourself. I want you, but not like this. I want you loving and embracing yourself and being a good mother. I know already that we both gon' have those fucked up days where our mental is off and that's okay too as long as we able to snap out of it and be there for one another. Feel me?" He let go of my hand and turned towards the window holding up his index finger at Jarei.

"Let me help you, I don't want help but if you willing to get help I will too. My parents got a family therapist. She annoying as hell but she's good at what she does. I'll take you back to the apartment I let you stay at. It's yours, I won't pop up or force myself on you. If it's time you need then you got that." His eyes were pleading with me. I slowly nodded my head.

"Okay." I agreed. "Thank you, Michael." I looked down at my red arms then back up at Michael. I would take his help and seek the help that I needed.

"I need you to turn the music up and turn your head. If you want, you can pray for this nigga's mercy." He smirked.

"Why?"

"Cause I'm about to beat this niggas ass and make him stay the fuck away from you. When I knock him out, I'm gon' go in that house and get your medicine since I know you ain't took it. You got a day to relax then you going back to work." I swallowed down hard and nodded again. Jarei needed his ass beat.

Michael calmly got out of the car and the first hit he delivered to Jarei rocked his entire world. He stumbled onto the grass and stood back up on shaky legs as Michael kept walking up to him calmly to pursue the ass whooping, he promised to give him. Something in me snapped as I opened my passenger door and got out the car.

The fresh air hit me; I took in a deep breath then approach them. Once I got to the side of Michael, I touched his arm then looked up into his cold gray eyes.

"I want him to feel how he made me feel twenty minutes ago. Go get some hot water and put it in a bucket." Michael gave me an evil smile and nodded as he turned towards Jarei who was now toothless.

"All I ever did was love you when I didn't even love myself. You constantly kicked me when I was down, never even trying to help me. When I constantly helped you and even took care of your ass!" I yelled at the top of my lungs.

"Fuck you bitch! You think this nigga gon' love you? He gon' treat you the same in a couple months-" Michael launched his fist back like he was Popeye and connected with Jarei's chin knocking him out instantly. Saying nothing, he walked towards the house and fifteen minutes later he came out holding a big pot of water. You could see it steaming. It looked like he actually boiled a pot of water which explained why it took him so long. Nyla walked out seconds later with a cold bottle of water and handed it to me. She looked at Jarei and shook her head. She turned on her heels and walked back into the house.

"Pour that cold water on him first." Michael coolly instructed. I took the top off and poured it all over him as he woke up gasping and struggling to breathe. Michael sat the pot of water down to bend down and rip Jarei's shirt off. Once it was off, he picked the big pot up, and tossed the water on Jarei causing him to scream out loud in agony.

"Let's go before I actually kill him right now. That voice in my head ain't agreeing with torture. It wants to murder." He walked away and I followed him closely. I didn't have shit else to say to Jarei's sick ass.

On the way to the apartment, I couldn't help myself from thinking about what Jarei tried to do to me. I couldn't believe that he really took things that far and tried to drown me in the tub. If it wasn't for Nyla, I wouldn't be here. Hell, if it wasn't for Michael coming to see about me when he did, I would probably be roaming the streets phoneless and broke trying to figure out where I was going.

"He tried to drown me." I blurted out just as Michael pulled in the front of his house. It was very quiet, and it looked like his house was the only house on the dead-end street. I didn't even bother to question him about why we were here. I thought he was taking me back to the apartment, but he didn't.

"I know, look at your pretty ass skin red and shit. I'm having my doctor come to look at you to make sure your skin isn't damaged. Then in the morning, Ms. Scott is coming to sit and talk with you. You raising a daughter, and these spells that you have of not washing your ass or feeling low of yourself ain't good." He got out of the car, and I wanted to ask him why he was so angry all of a sudden. It's like his mood did a quick three-sixty like something came to his mind. He didn't say anything to me as he opened the door to his truck and helped me out of the car. I was embarrassed but there was no running and hiding from the truth.

I walked closely behind Michael and took in his mini mansion. The two-story house looked like something right out of a magazine. The grass was green, and I was surprised to see beautiful roses going up the pathway to his front door. He stood in front of his door scanning his hand over some sort of scanner and the door opened up slowly for him.

"You can stay in the guest room down the hall to your left for the night. I won't bother you at all. When my doctor gets here, I'll knock at the door so he can come in and check you. If that's alright with you." He shut the front door behind me and gave me a cold look. His eyes still looked wild and dark. I could feel anger radiating off of him.

"What's wrong with you?" I looked up at him and when he didn't answer, I simply just waited for a response.

"You make my fuckin' heart itch Praylah, I don't like that feeling. You also just told me that a nigga just tried to drown you. Like really kill you, then you expect for me to let this nigga still breathe. You can't come in my life and rearrange some shit to your liking and expect me to have a good attitude about the shit." He left me standing there speechless as I stared at his muscular back. He took his winding staircase by two, with ease leaving me standing here dumbfounded.

Michael was a true character. I never asked him to get involved with any of my situations. I also didn't expect him to try to save me, but it was obvious that he felt like it was his duty to do so. This was another reason why I didn't want to stay in the apartment that he provided for me. I wasn't trying to come into his life and rearrange anything. The fact that he owned his own establishments and was rich scared me.

I read stories about rich men and the things they did with their money. It was a sea full of women, so I didn't know why he took a liking to me. Michael was also a killer; I saw the look in his eyes the way he handled Jarei. From his mental to the way he walked and talked had me intrigued but my conscious was constantly telling me to run for the hills and never look back. I was in for the ride of my life with this man. First step was explaining to him in the morning that I had changed my mind and planned on going to live with my parents or Era.

God, I hated how indecisive and wishy-washy I was. I couldn't make a solid decision to save my life but one thing I knew for sure was I didn't want to be depending on Michael.

SOULFUL HURTZ

"Soulful, when you coming home?" I hated hearing the worry in Luv's tone of voice. I hadn't been home in three weeks, not ready to fully face Jocelyn. I wanted to strangle her and make her feel the hurt that she caused me. Being a celebrity football player made it hard to move around like the street nigga I once was. Jocelyn had played me and played me well. The shit had me feeling sick to my stomach every single day.

I wasn't eating and I barely slept. I felt like a straight-up bitch but couldn't deny my own feelings and emotions. When a person you loved crossed you and showed disloyalty it sometimes made you question yourself. I tried to think of where I fucked up at with my wife. I respected her and never cheated up until Era and I was still wrong for that shit.

Jocelyn almost overdosing on the same shit that killed my mom had me pissed with her. What had me disgusted was her being so out of it that she didn't even know that her side nigga was carrying her to my front fucking door, looking at her with the same amount of love that I had for her ungrateful ass.

"I'll be by tonight; I got a game tomorrow. You and Passion should come to get out the house." Another fucked up thing was going through heartache and still having to work. When I was out on that field, I had to put all my personal issues to the side and give the game of football my all.

"Okay, I hope you talked to a lawyer." I could hear the attitude in Luv's voice.

"A lawyer for what?" I raised my brows.

"Divorce, you need to divorce her." My stomach did somersaults. I never even thought about divorce. I wasn't trying to be no simp ass nigga, but I loved Jocelyn. I felt like her cheating was my fault. I did get wrapped up in training and traveling for games. The way I easily cheated on her with Era from her not giving me the attention that I needed and not being supportive is probably why she cheated on me and started out on drugs. I didn't really know; this shit was confusing as fuck for me. I've never been through no shit like this.

I had everybody in my ear constantly telling me what I should and shouldn't do and knew I needed to figure this shit out on my own.

"Luv, mind your business. I'll see you in a few." I hung up not really trying to hear my sister and deal with her aggressive ass attitude that she always got. I started walking around the room and gathering my shit to get ready to go home. I couldn't keep running, it was time for me to face my wife and to see if anything between us was truly worth saving.

The house that Sovereign bought me was almost ready for me to move into. The contractors had a couple of last touches to add to it to my liking. I cruised home slowly, following the actual speed limits, something I never really did. I wasn't in a rush to get home because I had been running from having this conversation with Jocelyn.

I was a less confrontational person and whenever Jocelyn was in the wrong, she liked to yell and scream just to justify her actions. I wasn't with that shit; I was willing to admit my wrongs and find out what all she been hiding, and I needed to know why she did what she did. I didn't want excuses, I needed answers. Answers to why she felt the need to get on drugs and fuck another nigga.

I didn't have an excuse for her on why I fucked Era. I had an answer to that shit though. I didn't even know if it would happen again because from the time I saw Era, I had a strong attraction and connection with her that I didn't even have with my own wife from day one. That was the scary part, I had loyalty to Jocelyn, and I was willing to stick to it and stay away from Era.

That didn't mean that I couldn't stick to what I had offered Era and that was a chance. I felt like everyone deserved a chance, as Sovereign and Inferno gave to me. Era's voice was beautiful, and her looks were angelic. She was curvy as hell and her skin was so smooth, soft, and dark chocolate. She tasted even better, the mere thoughts that I had of her had my mouth watering.

Since I wasn't upfront with her, I asked Debo for her information and called Shelby Watts. I gave her all of Era's contact and social media handles. I didn't want shit in return but for her to really take off in her career. She had that same hungry look in her eyes that I had when I was determined to provide for my siblings.

Pulling up in front of my house, I took a deep breath and got out of my car. I kept my eyes glued to the front door, not really wanting to go inside. Before I could stick my key inside the door, Passion was opening the door up with her friends behind her.

"Hey Soul, me and my friends going to the mall." I nodded my head and hugged her tightly. Passion was quiet and a good girl, she was just sneaky as hell. Sometimes she went through gloomy days thinking about the foul things that our mother put us through. The toughest time that never left my brain was when I found her and my mom in a park. It also brought me back to a time when I stepped away from Jocelyn and from that particular time, I kicked myself in the ass for going back to her.

I got emotional as I went to take a seat on the couch and thought back to that night that changed me, and my sister's lives.

A slight grin spread across my face as I sat across from Jocelyn watching her look at the menu. We sat in a five-star steak house about to eat some good ass food. I couldn't believe how things turned from shit to sugar for me in a short period of time. My mom had been proving herself more and more each day. She stepped up with the girls and did her motherly thing with them. It left me a lot of time on my hands to step up with the gang and run things how it was supposed to be ran.

When Queen popped up with all of those drugs, we sat around the plastic folding table with crab legs and lobster tails, along with glasses of champagne celebrating new wealth to come. We had several new stash houses, so I didn't have to worry about hiding work in the same place that I laid my head at. I called a lot of shots and was still able to focus on school. I couldn't lie and say that I didn't want to be a part of school anymore. The way I saw it, in a couple of months things would be set straight for me. We would only make more money as time went on.

I stayed in school because it was my obligation to. I didn't want to disappoint Queen by dropping out and getting cocky. I was no dumb nigga, I wanted to still go to college and make something of myself. It just became hard to live a double life. I rubbed my hands down my fresh fade, and looked at Jocelyn, she looked so pretty and perfect. Her posture was perfect like a model. Today was Saturday and all I wanted to do was spend time with my girlfriend.

It felt like bitches knew I was on the come up, ever since I pulled up to school with my car and Jocelyn big cheesing in my passenger seat. I wasn't worried about none of them hoes because they weren't worried about this fat dusty nigga when I was really down bad. All the girls at school did was tear me down when I was already having it hard at home. Jocelyn never did me like that so for that reason alone a nigga was humble.

"We can share a Tomahawk steak and order some sides to share as well." Jocelyn closed the menu and looked up at me smiling. She was like a fresh breath of air; it made me happy just knowing she was happy with me.

"We ain't got to share shit Jah. Order what you want, I told you I was treating you today for your birthday." I got excited at the thought of her finally turning eighteen. I planned on leaving this restaurant and going home to get a change of clothes then taking her fine ass to a nice hotel and laying her down. I wasn't no virgin nigga; I had been fucking grown bitches since I was fifteen. Grown bitches were different, they didn't care about how I looked. They didn't see the bumps on my face and laugh. Their eyes traveled right down to my raggedy gray sweatpants and the big ass print that I had. I was packing and had a lot of dick to break a bitch down if I wanted to.

A lot of times the older bitches I fucked on was a means to me and my siblings having a home cooked meal. Thanks to Queen and all the facials and pimple popping she did, my face was starting to clear up. I still didn't feel a hundred percent confident with myself, but I liked the fact that I was now dressed better and all of them ugly ass bumps were slowly but surely disappearing.

"I like the new you." She picked up her strawberry lemonade and smiled bashfully.

"What was the old me like?" I wanted to know her viewpoint on how she felt about me, I knew she always looked my way but could never determine her thoughts about me. I assumed that she too thought I was a bum fat nigga with bad ass acne.

"The old you was shy, quiet... letting people treat you wrong. I saw pain every time your eyes met mine. The weight of the world on your shoulders. You really lived up to your last name, you were hurting bad." She reached across the table timidly and grabbed my hands. Picking my left hand up she pecked the rough side of my hand with her soft succulent lips. That shit did something to me, I didn't know what it felt like to receive affection and adoration, but Jocelyn was the female that had me experiencing a lot of things for the first time.

I remained quiet until the waitress came to the table to take our orders. We made small talk until our food arrived. After we ate and joked around, I found myself locked into my thoughts worried about taking my time with Jocelyn as far as laying her sexy body down and taking her down. I ain't never broke a girl's virginity, wasn't a soft bone in my body. I didn't know shit about making love, I didn't eat pussy because I wouldn't dare put my mouth on a random bitch.

All I did was hardcore fucking, enjoying the feeling of nutting in a condom then keep it pushing. With Jocelyn things had to be different. She was delicate and too beautiful to be treated like a slut.

"What you thinking about?" she asked as I pulled out a knot of cash and peeled a couple back to place into the small fob.

"You." I kept it short. I took in her diamond shaped face loving the way her curly natural lashes looked without her glasses on. I downed the rest of my drink, I wasn't broke, but I wasn't rich and wasting food and juice still wasn't an option for me. I knew what it felt like to not even have anything or nothing at all.

We left out the restaurant and I opened Jocelyn's door like the gentleman I tried to always be with her. Before she got into the car, I pulled her close to me. She placed her hand on my stomach and rubbed my round belly. That shit right there had me blushing and looking away from her.

"I can't wait to cuddle with you all night long." She tilted her head up and puckered her lips. This shit still felt too good to be true with this girl. She was just too damn good looking for a nigga like me. I bent down a little and aligned my lips with hers. I pecked her three times then just stared into her eyes.

"I hope you don't break a nigga's heart Jocelyn. I don't know how I'd react to that shit." I grabbed a handful of ass watching her blush and turn red in the cheeks.

"I hope you don't break mine either Soulful Hurtz. I know that dope boys got a lot of hoes." I put my nose in the crook of her neck enjoying the smell that came from her body.

"I ain't ya average dope boy, as long as I got you, I ain't worried bout no other bitch. I won me a trophy." I didn't know if it was corny as hell but soon as we got in the car, I connected my phone to the Bluetooth and played Future ft Kanye, "Trophy". We vibed on the freeway with my hand

39

holding hers as I controlled the steering wheel with one hand navigating to my house. I was so ready to get her to the hotel that I almost was about to say fuck going home.

I was a clean nigga and had to wash my ass every night so getting a change of clothes was a must. We pulled up to the projects, I parked close to the curb then helped Jocelyn out. The hood was jumping at seven p.m., it was the weekend, so shit was gon' be popping all night.

"I ain't gon' be long." I let Jocelyn know as I stuck my key in my door and let us in. I didn't mind her coming into the house, I rearranged some shit in the living room and had it looking way better. I opened the door and frowned when I didn't smell a home cooked meal. Luv sat on the new sectional couch that I had just bought watching the new fifty-inch TV that I got from Walmart.

"Luv, what I tell yo' lil ass bout watching Love and Hip Hop? It ain't for kids, put some other shit on." She smacked her lips then looked past me and smiled brightly at Jocelyn. She got up and hugged her as I surveyed the front of the house.

"Where Passion?" I asked Luv, Passion always ran into the living room from our room to greet me and tell me about her day.

"She went with momma to McDonald's, momma said she don't feel like cooking. We ate ice cream and hot Cheetos; they should be back in a minute." She flopped her little frail self back on the couch and flipped through the channels. I watched Jocelyn take a seat next to Luv on the couch. The both of them started talking, while I debated with myself. A part of me wanted to go back outside and hop in my whip to go find my mom and Passion. I didn't really like them walking around the projects. McDonald's was a ten-minute walk from the house. I shrugged it off

thinking that it was good for my moms and Passion to spend some alone time.

"How long they been gone?" I yelled over my shoulder, opening the door to my room.

"I don't know but they should be coming back." Luv yelled back. I opened the top drawer to my dresser and dug out a fresh pair of boxers along with a white beater. I went to the closet and got a fresh outfit for the next day. I planned on taking Jocelyn out to the Court Cafe in the morning. Tomorrow was a slow day since it was Sunday. I wanted all of us including my momma to go to the Pier and play games and walk on the beach.

Soon as I bent down to pick up my Nike backpack, I heard a loud boom. My heart immediately started to speed, I wanted to panic but I went right into protection mode. Throwing my backpack on the ground I heard muffled voices. I couldn't really make the voices out, but I could hear Jocelyn telling them that she didn't have any money. Frowning at her words, I snatched my gun from the top of the closet. I practically tip toed towards my room door.

Right now, I could hear the intruders fucking up the front of the house. They didn't come to harm anybody because I didn't hear them popping off at Jocelyn and Luv.

Hearing their footsteps come down the hallway, I pumped myself up. I was killing somebody today. I ain't have no drugs or no major cash here at this house no more. These project niggas probably thought I had money now since I was pushing a car. They thought they were 'bout to catch me slipping but that wasn't fenna be the case here tonight. Queen gave me my own personal stash spot since we had more dope to move.

No longer able to waste any more time for the sake of my sister and Jocelyn's safety I popped out in the hallway shooting first watching two bodies drop. I delivered a head shot to the first tall body that was bulky. The second person turned their back in the middle of me shooting them, they collapsed hard onto the carpet.

"F.Y.F mutha fuccas." I moved towards them and kicked their guns away from their hands. Snatching the ski mask off the first nigga, I squatted down stunned as fuck.

"I knew this nigga was moving foul." I shook my head. Hawking up spit, it landed on his face. The second body caught my attention, it was the voice that stalled me.

"Murk'um." She simpered and struggled with turning over.

"Jah take my sister and go to your house!" I yelled; Luv was probably traumatized enough from them busting up in here.

"You fat muthafucka!" Her voice sounded like she was gargling mouthwash. Coughing up blood, I moved towards her and turned her over, removing the ski mask.

"What the fuck you on Clapback?" I felt betrayed and confused as fuck. Her eyes were starting to roll back as her body convulsed. Panic surged through me. I never had problems with Clapback, I always thought she was weird for fucking on Murk'um but didn't judge her for that shit. It wasn't my place to insert myself in nobody's business if it didn't concern my money.

"Fuck!" I stood up and fished for my phone in my pockets. I dialed Queen because I truly didn't know what to do. She answered on the second ring and said nothing as usual.

"Queen, I killed Murk'um and umm your sister Clapback, I shot in the back or somewhere I don't really know man! Fuck! Her body convulsing and it ain't looking too good. They broke into my apartment with ski mask on, I don't know what this shit about Queen and I don't know what to do."

"You must be drunk." She chuckled nervously. "I'm gon' send someone to check on you, take your medicine, and go lay down. Rest Teddy, stop talking so crazy." She hung up leaving me standing there confused as fuck. I sat down on my couch; I didn't even bother to look at the bodies in the hallway. It felt like I was stuck in a bad dream. Shit just went left fast as fuck. My nerves were rattled bad, if I killed Queen's sister then I didn't know where that would leave us. Queen changed my life; I just didn't know what to make of all of this at this very moment.

After sitting there for fifteen minutes, I heard cars pulling up. I still didn't move, I just stayed seated wondering what the fuck my fate was gone be. I didn't feel defeated, so I kept my chin up. I was protecting my girl and little sister. I didn't know what the fuck Murk'um and Clapback was on. Queen taught me to always shoot first and ask questions later.

A crew of five men in all black with gloves and masks walked in first. They said nothing and walked right towards the hallway. After a couple of seconds three more men walked in, two of them had menacing scowls on their faces. The one in the front didn't look bothered at all, he held a flamethrower in his right hand. In his left hand was a thick Cuban cigar. He looked like he was a mixed nigga. Something about him was dark, his eyes looked icy as fuck.

"I'm Inferno, Queens husband. While my men work, I'll take a seat and explain somethings to you." One of his men followed him to the couch, the other nigga walked to where the men were working, one picked up Murk'um's body.

"Fuck, tell me do the bitch got a pulse. Pussy too good to be dead man." The dude that walked in with Inferno stood over Clapback like he was pissed.

"There's a faint pulse." One of the workers said.

"Good, get her to our doctors, make sure you tell them

she has to survive. My wife wouldn't know what to do without this treacherous bitch. I will let her decide her fate." He looked at me as a long stream of ashes hit the carpet.

"Killa get over here, we are in the middle of conducting business." Inferno's voice was flat void of any emotion.

"First body?" He raised a brow; I shook my head yes still unable to speak. He sat up in the love seat across from me and smirked, but that shit looked like he was sneering at me.

"Understandable, Queen wanted to be here. She's in Mexico, I was getting ready to head there too. Until she called." He never broke eye contact as he took a deep pull from his cigar and then released the smoke.

"You made a big mistake tonight, well, actually two mistakes Teddy. One mistake was not delivering two head-shots to your intruders. Second mistake was calling on an unprotected phone line admitting to the crime you did."

"I'm sorry, I wasn't thinking." He pointed to the phone still sitting in my hand, I passed it to him and watched him squeeze it with one hand until the screen shattered in his hands. He tossed it on the floor and held his free hand out as the big nigga behind him handed him a clear bottle that looked like it had water inside.

"I'll be moving your location; this spot will be burned down to the ground." He popped the cap off and poured the clear liquid onto the already broken phone.

"No need to worry, my men moving all of the important things that your household needs." He picked up his flamethrower and squeezed what looked like a trigger. Flames shot out and caught onto the phone as it began to burn slowly. Inferno started to talk again but he looked like he was stuck in a trance watching the small fire before us.

"Big B is the big nigga behind me, he will give you the address of where you will be staying. Queen will not return

44

until three to four days and she will break the news to your crew on what happened and decide what explanation to give. When I caught my first body, I burned them until there was nothing, but bones left. I didn't sleep for a whole week until I went and bought some sleeping pills. Not saying that it's going to make it better. When you catch your first body it sticks with you more than the bodies that come afterwards. It's like the soul of the first body you take follows you around in life taunting you like you can't or won't kill again. I proved that first soul wrong every single time I killed a person. It's kind of like training your conscience to believe in what you feel is right. Don't fret the situation to hard young man, you did what you was supposed to. Only next time, you learn from this and never miss your mark."

He stood up as I let his words sink in, something inside of me felt weird as hell. It felt like I wasn't even breathing normally. By the time they had the suburban truck loaded up with all of our personal belongings, I walked out of the house slowly turning around to see Big B walking out the house with lighter fluid leaking from the bottle. He drenched the three steps that led to the front door as Inferno took his flamethrower and placed it down on the front doorstep. Security stood around us blocking us from the nosey ass neighbors that was most likely watching.

The cold breeze made the fire travel faster until the whole project unit was set ablaze. Inferno watched for a couple of minutes and shook his head.

"I wish I could stay and watch the fire take this place all the way down, but I have to move out. Get your family and go to the address Big B gives you." He turned and walked off with one hand stuffed in his pocket, his free handheld on to his flamethrower. The nigga was insane, his calm nonchalant presence was evident as he waved bye from the back window.

It hit me then that my mom and Passion hadn't made it home just yet.

"Fuck!" I shook my head in defeat, I couldn't stay stagnant. I was going to have to go look for my mom and sister. There was no way she up and went to fucking McDonald's it had been over an hour now and I knew that Luv and Jocelyn were now worried. I got the keys and address from Big B then jumped in my car to go find my mom and Passion first.

In the pits of my stomach, I felt something wasn't right. Fear soared throughout my body, and I found it ironic how I was saying a silent prayer to God after I just killed a nigga. I just hope that God would listen to me because I would lose my cool if something happened to my little sister or momma.

I drove block after block stopping to ask a couple of people that I saw hanging out if they saw my mom. Each person said no, I was losing hope wondering where the fuck could she possibly be. I knew like hell that my mom wouldn't ever possibly think to go get high while she was out with my sister. Something inside of me forced me to face the facts. The raw truth of who my mom was. Sure, she got her act together over the past couple of weeks and did the motherly thing. Antoinette still had her nights where she would stumble in, reeking of alcohol and pass out on the couch mumbling, but I didn't think she was still using due to the next morning. She would wake up and get the girls ready for school.

I didn't ask her questions because she was grown as hell. I was already blaming myself for everything. I got so caught up in hustling and trying to provide that I didn't pay closer attention. I felt overwhelmed and out of control of what was probably going on. After praying again, a thought popped up in my head. When my mom would disappear for days and I would get worried for her, I would go searching for her at a particular park.

Senseta Park had nothing but junkies and homeless people. It was located on the outside of the projects. Up-and-coming dope boys would hang out there and make the most money because junkies kept coming up to them to get high. Their crack was stepped on a million times making the junkies want more and more product. Junkies would run out of money and perform sinful acts like stealing from their loved ones and even pimping out their fucking kids to the perverted dope boys just to get high for ten minutes. I didn't want to go to Senseta because I knew if I went there and saw my sister in such a fucked-up environment, I would never be able to forgive my mom.

I pulled right into the park's parking lot and grabbed my gun from the glove compartment. Trash littered the grass and the air smelled like drugs, piss, and shit. I started from the front of the park and worked my way through. Checking the park restrooms, I came up empty handed. Feeling hopeless I turned to walk back to my car until I heard a loud scream. That scream belonged to Passion. It was the same scream she had when she saw a rat during wintertime in our apartment.

It was so dark that the only light that helped my vision was the streetlights. Pulling up my jeans, I picked my pace up until I reached the park's gym. I could hear a bunch of talking and laughing followed by my sister crying. My adrenaline was on a hundred as I pulled my gun from my waist. Making my way to the back of the gym, I ran to my sister that was being held down by two fiends and snatched her up while pointing my gun.

"Their hurting her Soulful! She's dead! Mommy is dead!" She held onto my neck so tightly it felt like she was choking me. I stood tall with her and pushed a couple of fiends out my way so I could see what their attention was on.

My eyes had to be deceiving me, my heart instantly broke

for the second time out of my life as I watched my mother's limp body get pounded from the back. The dope boy held the top of her forehead as he thrusted in and out of her, the grunting noises had me nauseated. I couldn't think straight as I picked my gun up and blew his fucking brains out. Passion screamed again, bringing me back to reality as all the fiends scattered away like roaches. My mom laid on the concrete looking lifeless as Passion cried her little heart out in my arms. Just within two hours, I caught another body. Only this time, I didn't give a fuck about the body I just dropped. I placed Passion to her feet and checked my moms for a pulse. Once I felt one, I picked her up and carried her to my car. After tonight, I didn't want shit to do with her. I planned on taking my sisters far the fuck away and providing for them the best way I knew how.

I couldn't focus on school or Jocelyn; I was here to grind hard and provide for my sisters. I couldn't be wishing on a fucking star trying to pray for my momma to get clean, when she constantly made stupid ass decisions like the choice she made tonight. Once I got Passion and my mom in the car, I stopped by a pay phone to call Jocelyn. I needed her to bring Luv on the next block so I could take her to the address that Big B provided. I didn't want to take the chance of hitting the projects and running into the police when I still didn't have a driver's license.

"You, okay?" Jocelyn asked me as she tried to search my eyes. I struggled with looking into her beautiful eyes because I knew that I was about to hurt her. It was never my intention to do so though.

"Yea, I'm straight. Thanks for looking out for Luv." I looked back at the car and could still see my mom knocked out. Passion had a haunted look in her eyes that pained my soul.

"I still can come with you; my mom is gone with her boo for the weekend." She smiled and placed her hand on my arm. It amazed me how calm she was after she heard and saw what went on back at my house. Then again if you lived in the projects, you became immune to certain shit. Like niggas robbing you and watching a few bodies drop around you. Jocelyn's brother was a hitta so she knew how shit went.

"Nah, but listen Jah, you free to move on. I got some heavy shit I'm dealing with and you probably ain't gon' see a nigga for a while." She shook her head no, and I let out a breath that I had been holding. Licking my dry lips, all I could see was the bodies I dropped tonight. Just like that, I forgot all about the good time I had with Jocelyn. I forgot about how she calmed me and felt good for my soul.

"Let me be there for you Soulful, please?" I wanted to say yes but I couldn't put that type of burden on her. I stepped back, preparing to turn away from her. I had been standing here too long and my mom needed medical attention. I didn't know what tomorrow would be like or how things would be with Queen and I since Clapback was now on her deathbed. Although I had every right to shoot her sister, that was still her flesh and blood. I knew the great measures that I would take for my little sisters right or wrong. I could only hope that I still had a chance to be on Queen's team.

"I got to go Jah." I turned to walk away, and she grabbed my hand, pulling me to her, she grabbed a hold of my shirt and tried to pull me closer to her. She stood on her tippy toes struggling to reach my lips. I finally gave in and moved down to her lips and kissed her passionately before releasing her. She had tears welled up in her eyes and I had tears pouring from my soul. I often wondered why my life was so fucked up. Every time shit looked up to a nigga some bad shit had to happen that would pull me back down into that deep depres-

sion that I had to fight with just to stay sane for my sisters that fully depended on me.

"Promise me that you will come and see about me when you straight. If you ever need me Soulful, I will be right here for you." I nodded my head and turned to walk away from her. Each step that I took felt heavier than the last. I got in the car and embraced the silence. I drove twenty miles to a good hospital and carried my mom in through the entrance. I laid her down in the chair and took a good long look at her.

Backhanding the tears that had fallen down my face, I could barely recognize her. I saw her in the light and got mad all over again. She had knots all over her forehead and her lips were swollen as well. It looked like her nose was broken; her brown body had bruises all over. The purple maxi dress she had on was ripped and exposing some of her lady parts. Niggas had violated my momma bad but not how she violated Passion by putting her in that predicament.

Yelling out for the concierge to come help her and send my momma a doctor, I walked out of the hospital with blurry eyes and a heavy heart. I remembered what Jocelyn told me and agreed a hundred percent. My mom knew what she was doing, naming me Soulful Hurtz. I had a permanent feeling of hurt embedded inside of me. I didn't see that shit going away no time soon.

SOULFUL HURTZ

$\mathcal{I}$ wiped my face so much to quickly wipe the tears away that my cheeks were burning. I knew I had small welts on my face from the heavy rings on my fingers. I backhanded my face so much to attempt to stop the tears because I didn't want to risk Luv or Jocelyn catching me having a weak-ass moment.

I was the man of this house and never wanted to show weakness. I allowed myself to have my moments and let them go. Little things triggered me, like my sister's, especially Passion. Seeing how far we all came and what wealth brought us was amazing. I remember when that night took place and I found Passion and my mom in that park. Passion just wasn't the same. She lost her glow, and she wasn't as vibrant, she didn't even talk much for a long time after that.

Passion would one word us and stay in her room until Sovereign got her out of that. My sisters and I were very humble and grateful. We didn't take advantage of the fact that we were now wealthy. We had our ups and downs, but we still made sure to love on one another. Since we didn't have parents or much family we stuck together and they respected me as their leader, guardian, and someone they could be open with.

"Are you going to leave me?" I turned to see Jocelyn walking in the front room looking timid and tired. She had bags around her eyes like she hadn't slept much, she looked how she did when she first learned that her brother was murdered.

"It all depends, Jah. Seems like we both wrapped up in our own shit. You hurt the fuck out of me and I'm getting ready to hurt you. That's if you even give a fuck." I shook my head and just looked into her pretty ass face. Even with weight loss, Jocelyn was still beautiful as fuck.

Grabbing the throw blanket, she wrapped herself up with it and sat down across from me and I decided to start first.

"I cheated on you the night you almost overdosed." I stopped talking to gauge her reaction. Her face remained neutral, and she didn't show any emotion.

"I know you were cheating Soulful. It's what rich niggas do that is why I had Dmack." She shrugged then looked under her nail bed and flicked away invisible dirt. I kept myself calm the best way I knew how and continued this conversation that I was already tired of before it even started good.

"How long you been fucking that nigga?" I looked into her eyes to see if she would tell the truth. Whenever Joceyln lied, her eyes shifted all around and she couldn't maintain eye contact to save her life.

"Two years, it's how I got hooked on cocaine. He started falling in love with me and stopped selling it to me so I went to another guy that I met at a club and copped from him."

"Two years Jah? I never fucking cheated on you, bro, only once. Fuck the money and fuck the fame! I've been dedicated and loyal to you ma. Why the fuck you play a nigga so hard yo'?" My throat burned and I felt a lump forming in my throat as I constantly tried to clear my passageway.

"Oh, please Soul! All you care about is those bad ass sisters and Sovereign! Let me not leave out gay ass Berto. There's no telling if you fucking him or Sovereign." She spat as I stood to my feet and halted my steps when I realized for the first time ever, I wanted to slap the light freckles off her fuckin' face. I chuckled angrily and placed my hands behind my back and started pacing right in front of her.

"Jocelyn, don't disrespect me again, keep my sisters out yo' fuckin' mouth and never disrespect my manhood again before you find yourself dead like that bitch ass nigga that carried yo' coke head pitiful ass up to my doorstep." She finally showed emotion, that neutral face of hers cracked and her eyes instantly welled up with tears.

"Soulful, you didn't... I know you did not kill Dmack!" her voice elevated as her tears fucked me up even more. Was my wife sitting here crying over the next nigga when it felt like she wouldn't even fight for us?

"Jah, you forget how the fuck I am. What I come from and most definitely what I'm about." I said in a chill tone.

"You thought another drug dealing nigga was gon' come to my house, private property where I rest my head... where my sisters rest their head, kiss my wife on the lips and enter my fuckin' home! You really thought in ya fucked up mind that this nigga was gon' be able to live and tell the tale bitch!"

"I'm in love with him Soulful but I love you!!! Why did you fucking kill him!" She sobbed, and I stopped pacing and casually walked up to the big canvas picture of me and her on our wedding day and snatched it off the wall. I purposely tossed it her way knowing it was going to miss her by a couple of inches. The glass shattered making her jump hard.

"Get the fuck out Jah." The way she was making me feel

was crazy as fuck. How was I supposed to process this shit? A woman that I fell in love with was actually in love with another man, a dead one at that.

"I can't leave, you're all me and my baby has now Soulful! You made my baby a bastard child." She sniveled and simpered hard. I looked over at her in disbelief. This time I didn't even stop my own tears. The weight of her words weighed me down so hard that I took a bow until I was on bended knee with my head in my hands. Fuck, she got me down bad.

"Pregnant? With another nigga baby Jah?" I shook my head as I felt my chest constricted hard. A sharp pain hit me as I kept my head bowed, I couldn't find the strength to even look at her. This the weakest a person ever had me feeling. This couldn't be the woman that I crushed hard on in high school. The popular chick that even gave me the time of day when I was fat and ugly with not even five dollars to my name. Nah this just couldn't be her right now.

The old Jocelyn never gave up on me, she knew just how much I went through. She knew the real me and how hopeful I was back then of us and my mom getting and staying sober. This wasn't the Jocelyn I knew back in the days of poverty. Money had to have changed who she was, and I just couldn't fathom that. My mind went back to the day Jocelyn approached me when I was on the way home with a bag full of dope.

I already knew I was going to make her mine besides her already having a nigga.

I noticed Jocelyn sitting on her steps while her lame ass nigga got his mack on with her. We locked eyes and I kept pushing past until she called out to me.

"Teddy!" I stopped but didn't turn around to face her. I

could smell her strawberry scent approaching and finally turned to face her.

"Yea?" I eyed her down, I slightly pulled my hoodie back a little and looked over her shoulder looking directly at her nigga that mugged me hard. He mouthed 'dusty ass nigga' and I winked at him. If he got stupid, I had no problem blowing his head off, to protect the dope and money I had in my backpack.

"I thought you were walking me home so we could go over all the missing assignments. You know, Soul... if you don't make up these assignments then you can't finish out the year playing football."

"Fuck football, I got plays and moves to make. I'll walk you home tomorrow and we can do the assignments though." I hiked my backpack up. I didn't want to really disappoint her but the only thing I gave a fuck about right now was making ends meet. The only reason why I stayed in school was because Queen insisted that I go. She paid a grip too. I didn't like the uppity ass private school nor the kids there. It felt like I was too grown to even be there even though I was turning eighteen really soon.

"Right, don't let this street shit suck you in, Soulful. I want to help you." She softly said as her eyes batted at me. Her smell was intoxicating as fuck, and I had to remind myself that a girl like Jocelyn would never fuck with a dirty nigga like me.

"I appreciate you; I'll see what I can do. Get back to your nigga, the way he looking at me got me uncomfortable." I was on go and I already heard all about that nigga. He was a stick-up kid, all the jewelry that was on him had been stolen. I didn't want to chance having to pop her nigga.

"Okay but wait for me tomorrow, after school Soulful." She gave me that innocent smile and pulled her glasses up.

Touching my forearm softly, she turned and walked away, right into that nigga's arms. I got pissed when he grabbed a handful of ass and winked at me. I couldn't help the angry chuckle that left my mouth. I turned and finished the ten-minute walk to my house.

Arriving home, I stopped at the door when I heard music and good smelling food. It felt too good to be true if it was my mom up in here throwing down like she used to back when I was younger. I let myself in and couldn't hide my smile. My sisters greeted me and got back to doing their thing which was sitting on the couch watching TV. They looked content with their pajamas on and for once they weren't asking me what was for dinner.

I walked out of the living room and into the kitchen. My mom had music playing as she took some fried chicken out the frying pan and put it on a paper plate that was laced with paper towels to catch the grease. When she looked at me, she was sober, and I could see the sparkle in her eyes. I was tired as hell and felt relieved that I didn't have to put together another nasty meal. The kitchen and living room were clean and it smelled damn good. I embraced my mom tight to show her my appreciation and then went to the back to hide my dope until tomorrow. I just silently prayed that she kept this shit up. Me and the girls needed her more than she knew. I would hustle from sunup to sundown to provide for my mom and sisters just to have my momma home and drug free. The logical and negative side of me knew that it wouldn't be long before she left and went back to the streets. My mom was the first and only woman that kept repeatedly breaking and ripping a niggas heart out.

Jocelyn was now the second woman to break my heart and I didn't know if I could or would ever recover from this shit. I finally found my strength and looked up into her face.

"Jah, rather you believe me or not. I never cheated on you. My first-time cheating was a couple of weeks ago. I was wrong as fuck for that shit too. I did it and I guess it was because I was missing intimacy from you. I missed when you were there for me and cheering me on like I've always cheered for you. I always stayed planted and loyal to you through it all even when it felt like it was too much. I don't even know what to say, but just know you really fucked me up. You fucked me up so bad and I can't even deny how hurt I am right now." I sighed and finally stood up to my feet.

"I'm so loyal of a nigga that even though you did me wrong as fuck ma, I won't turn my back on you entirely. I'll pay for your divorce lawyer and mine and you can keep this house and get whatever spousal shit that I know you gon' go after." I turned away and walked towards the long hallway that led to the steps to get me to my room. I stopped walking when a thought crossed my mind.

"If you even think about going to talk to the police, I mean, if I even think that you thinking 'bout running your mouth on that nigga Dmack disappearance then best believe I'm gon' relieve you of all your worries and fears by sending you and that baby right with him." With that I walked away with a heavy mind and heart.

ERA

J stifled a yawn and looked out the booth I was standing in. The time read five am. For a week and a half, I had been in grind mode. I already had recorded songs that Shelby got mixed and put out and advertised on big platforms. She had my EP mixed and mastered and plastered everywhere for the world to hear. I still had to second-guess because Devin was in the back of my mind.

I know by now he knew and heard of me going viral. I was waiting for him to work his magic and get it all shut down. That wasn't the case so far and I was grateful for that. It's really crazy how Shelby knew exactly what to do to get my name out there. She kept saying that she wanted me viral on every social media platform within twenty-four hours and sis wasn't lying because I was viral as hell.

Even my next-door neighbors were congratulating me, and I didn't know exactly for what because I wasn't even a signed artist. Shelby stated that I didn't need a record company to solidify my place in the industry. If I followed the steps, she provided she claimed that I could remain an independent artist and own all masters and royalties which sounded good as hell to me.

I asked her how much I owed her because everything had a fee. Shelby let me know that her services had been covered and that when I made it big, I could decide if I still wanted to work with her as my manager. She said by then I would be bringing in the big bucks and I could decide how much I felt she was worth. So far, in my eyes, Shelby Watts was worth a lot because in just under two weeks she had my name buzzing. Sis wasn't nothing to play around with and she had proven that in such a short time frame.

I blinked my burning eyes and looked out the booth waiting for the engineer to give me the signal. The beat finally dropped, and I caught the beat and let my voice soar. Just like that I was already in my element. I was finishing up an album that I never seemed to find time to complete being stuck with bills and finding the time to get into a good studio. I only had six more songs to write and complete, Shelby had me so pumped that soon as I got off work, I was headed straight home to write and listen to beats that she emailed me.

I was tired but pushed myself because I knew this was something that I really wanted. It was a dream of mine that I envisioned since a little girl. I had black circles forming around my eyes, I had only been functioning off a few hours of sleep for the past week. I'd get up every day at three in the morning shower and spend at least two hours in the studio. After the studio, I'd grab breakfast and head right to the restaurant to open up and oversee things.

My co-workers did a wonderful job at making things easier for me, so on my down time, I found myself in the back where my office was writing music. Soon, when the money started to roll in, I saw myself quitting but for now I needed all the money

I could get so less sleep was the sacrifice to getting to where I needed to be. Shelby stood behind the engineer smoking a blunt while looking down intently at the mixing board.

She reached over and pressed a button to stop the track as I stifled a yawn not really wanting to show them how tired I was.

"Sounds a little flat Era, come out and drink some coffee then go back in." She walked towards the couch and took a seat. Shelby was in her late forties and her persona screamed hood, but she knew how to get right down to business and conduct herself very professionally. I picked up my feet and made my way out the booth and took a seat right behind the mixer watching the engineer play around with buttons and replay the track. Picking up the coffee mug, I took slow sips as Shelby ashed her blunt and took another long tote.

"I got some good news and slightly bad news." She smiled big, making me smile. I ignored the fact that she even had bad news to mix in with her good news. I was learning Shelby in the short amount of time that I met her. She loved saying she had good and bad news. Her bad news always consisted of the time frame of things which wasn't always bad. I could adapt and make things work.

"B.E.T. want you to perform to fill in the artist that backed out at the last minute. It's very last minute and you haven't even established yourself yet in the industry. Understand what I told you though, one viral moment on social media can take whatever career you want to heights you never thought. You have millions of views and that takes most artists weeks to acquire. We have to jump on this and take advantage now. Watch, after this performance, your business email will be blowing up with proposal sharks. Record labels begging for your time and attention."

I swallowed down hard as tears of joy stung my eyes. I

didn't think I heard her correctly. Not B.E.T., a channel I grew up watching and fantasizing about being on. I looked at her like what she was saying wasn't real.

"I don't even know what to say… is Soulful behind all of this?" I didn't know what made me ask that, but it was in the back of my mind, and the thought of him being behind such a big thing made me think of Devin. Devin felt like he had so much control and I didn't want another man thinking he could take my dream away from me so they could shit all over me.

"CHILE, he's been paying for this state-of-the-art studio time. Everything else is all me. If you want to know, he paid me a hefty amount of money. I asked him was it because he liked you and if he wanted something in return. He knows I don't get in between dick and pussy favors or business." My chest constricted with how straight to the point she was.

"HIS ANSWER WAS, he felt like you were too good to be working in a restaurant when your voice sounded like it was touched by an angel. He also emphasized how beautiful you were, he said you had the voice and the look and that…" she looked away as her face went through a series of emotions.

"HE SAID that we could give each other a big break. Listen Era, I don't know you and Soulful's situation, but he has always been a good friend to me. I've been in different industries, and I have been used, abused, and my name tarnished a couple of times. I have the tools and connections, if you make it, I make it and I promise I will stick to you like glue if you will let me." She laughed a little. "I once had a man that black balled me so when you told me that on our first time talking, I felt connected to you in a way. I know what that pain feels like. That's not a story for me to tell right now. All I know is that even though Soulful initiated us meeting. I will never turn away from you if he decides to speak and say some shit although I know he won't. Soulful is very thorough and a hundred percent loyal." I shook my head at that because he wasn't loyal to his wife from what I gathered.

He said the right things to me and made me feel special even though it was a one-night stand. The way he rushed out that room crushed me even though I knew it shouldn't. It made me realize how stupid and naive I was being laying down with a stranger. I didn't bother telling Soulful what Devin did to me, hell I never even had the time to express that to him because it was a one-time encounter.

"I TOLD YOU, girl, this shit was gon' move fast. One viral moment and you will become even more known appearing on B.E.T. Let's bask in that and keep pushing." I smiled and nodded my head. I was ready, all this hard work was going to pay off one way or the other.

"THE BAD NEWS IS… it's this weekend. Tomorrow, we have to skip our evening studio time. I need you to leave work early to find the perfect gown and start rehearsing a couple of songs from your EP." My heart started beating fast, my stomach started cramping from nervousness. I thought of my mom and uncles and giving them the good news. Then my anxiety got the best of me thinking about seeing my mom in the crowd with tears of joy in her eyes being proud of me.

. . .

"THANK YOU, SHELBY." I took another sip of coffee.

"THANK THE MIC, GON' get in that booth and sing from the stomach up to your heart girl." I nodded my head and did just as she said.

* * *

"GIRL I'M SPRUNG, like the real kind!" I looked over at Ju'well and shook my head. Her and Honor had become close, and I was actually happy seeing my friend so pumped up and happy.

"I can tell you don't call me for our three-way calls. Hell, not even Pray." I rolled my eyes and looked at the time. I didn't want to sound like I was complaining but we all seemed too busy for each other. Pray was wrapped into settling in her place with Heaven and her parents up her back. Not only that, Jarei's bitch ass was now secretly threatening to take her to court for Heaven out of spite. I told her not to even worry about that asshole. He didn't even have a legal job and barely wanted to be a father. I kept convincing her that Jarei was nothing more but a bitter ass baby daddy mad that another man stepped up and was now doing what he should have been doing.

SPEAKING OF PRAYLAH, she walked in looking sluggish and out of touch. She had been coming to work every day, but it seemed like she was super depressed. I didn't want to press her, but my patience was growing thin. She promised me that it wasn't Debo and told me and Ju'well that Debo was actually giving her the space to heal. He didn't pop up or come over unless she called him. What I could say is that he upgraded my girl tremendously.

HER THREADS of clothing were nice as hell and her once kinky red fro was in some nice small knotless braids going past her curvy backside.

"I WANT to see that spark in your eyes friend. Not that dull shit, you waking up each day is enough to feel blessed and smile." I gave her a serious look hoping my good news would hype her up.

"JAREI IS GETTING in my parents head now, trying to get them to believe that my mental is way off and that I'm not fit to watch or have my baby." She dropped her shoulders in defeat and stared off into space.

"THEY DON'T EVEN KNOW about how that fucker tried to murder me, drown me alive and my only saving grace was Nyla out of all fucking people. I'm still stuck on that Era. I gave my all loving Jarei, literally my all. For him to paint this vivid fake picture is hurting me bad. I feel even more like shit for not really talking and getting to know Michael. I'm just scared of love at this point."

. . .

I TOOK a step back and leaned on my desk, my hands became clammy as I looked at Praylah with a new understanding.

"MURDER YOU?" My words came out clipped because I was attempting to take deep breaths to really grasp what she had just said.

"WHAT THE FUCK you mean he tried to murder you?" Ju'well harshly whispered loudly like someone was nearby listening.

"HE GOT MAD; I was in my depressed state of mind. The state of mind when I don't do shit for myself but exist. I hadn't bathed or even ate, just watching Jr. and dealing with Nyla living there. He ran hot bubble bath water and was saying all kinds of shit and threw me in the hot ass water and started dunking and holding my head underneath the water. Nyla saved me but...." She broke down and my heart cracked. My anger rose so high that I felt dizzy. Ju'well's caramel cheeks were beet red. We looked up at each other and communicated with our eyes.

I HAD HEARD ENOUGH, I looked at my watch and noticed it was Ju'well break time and I also had free time.

"JU'WELL LET'S TAKE A RIDE." I calmly said. Praylah eyes looked like they were getting ready to pop out of socket.

· · ·

"WHAT? WHERE Y'ALL GOING?" She looked confused and scared at the same time.

"TO BEAT THAT NIGGA ASS! I'm calling my momma too! I think it's safe to say we all tired of this nigga. I gave him so many passes for you out of respect but now it's up and fucking stuck like the clouds on a rainy day! I can't believe you didn't let Debo off that nigga!" I was so pissed that I didn't realize my voice going up a couple of notches. Snatching my purse and stomping out my office with them following close behind me. I gave instructions to my staff letting them know that we would be back in an hour.

I HEADED out of the restaurant with Praylah begging me and Ju'well to stop. I ignored her ass and texted my mom letting her know to meet me at Praylah's old house that her and Jarei shared. The whole ride there I hit my vape pen that I kept in the middle console. I cursed myself because I told Shelby that I would quit so that the vape didn't end up affecting my voice. Right now, my nerves are bad, and I had so much anger flowing through me.

I COULDN'T BELIEVE Jarei attempted to take the mother of his child out. Praylah sat in the back seat biting her nails and mumbling things that I couldn't really make out. I looked over at Ju'well and chuckled a little. My girl was always down for whatever. Right now, she was gathering all of her passion twists and placing it into a high bun at the top of her head. She unbuttoned the top button to her uniform shirt and cracked her neck.

. . .

IT TOOK us about thirty minutes with L.A.'s terrible traffic to pull up to the house. The first person that I spotted was Jarei's ol' dusty ass standing next to a nigga on the porch smoking a blunt. He used his right hand as a visor to block the sun to squint and smile at my car. My crazy ass smiled right back at him as excitement started to twist all around inside of me.

"WE BOUT to jump this nigga, Praylah you gon' step to. I want you to think about all the times he cheated and left you at home with both his kids. All the name calling and treating you fucked up. Most of all he tried to take you from your baby by killing you. Nah, fuck all of that bullshit! You fenna get pay back on this nigga and boss the fuck up!" She quickly nodded her head just as my momma pulled up all crazy. I could've sworn her BMW SUV was nearly on two wheels.

MY MOM PULLED ALL the way into the driveway with her baby deuce deuce out. I was surprised she didn't pop up with my uncles. She had a blunt between her lips still burning, her hair was protected in a bonnet. We hurried and got out of the car before my mom took the lead and showed all the way out, but it was a little too late.

"BOY, BOY, BOY! I BEEN MUTHAFUCKIN' waiting for either Praylah or my daughter to call me and tell me to come through this muthafucka!" Each step she took her big breast bounced all over the place like Madea.

. . .

"Boy, Boy BOYYYYYA! What you gotta say boy!?" My mom had that deranged look in her eyes as I stepped to the side of her. She had no clue what was going on and that made me smile. I really wanted to burst out laughing because it really made no sense how my mom stayed on go. Her eyes quickly scanned over me and Praylah's faces to make sure we were okay and hadn't been touched.

"Ms. Earlene, I don't want no problems. You overstepping boundaries right now." Jarei stepped off the porch with his eyes glued to Praylah. "That nigga dressing you up and shit, got ya hair done up. How long this gon' last before you start skipping baths and acting how you really act? Where the fuck my daughter at Praylah?" He tried to step closer to her and that's when I stepped chest to chest to him.

"Nigga you ain't in the position to ask no questions." My top lip curled.

"You show in the fuck not. We ain't got much time either, so let's get to why we here." Ju'well urged.

"You tried to drown my best friend, tried to kill her and belittle her when she was already feeling low enough." My voice cracked a little just thinking about Praylah feeling help-less cause of this bitch ass nigga.

.   .   .

"NIGGA YOU ACTING like she ain't got nobody else besides her daughter and yo' phony ass to love on her. We sat back long enough and now we here, nigga. So be about all of that shit in front of us right now." Ju'well urged Jarei as he chuckled like something was hilarious to him.

"YOU KNOW WHAT JU'WELL, you absolutely right." I fake acted like I was walking away but swiftly turned back around and used all my strength to knee Jarei right in his funky jewels.

"BITCH! AHHHHH!" Ju'well lifted her small ass foot and kicked him in his chin making him stumble back. I looked at Praylah and nodded my head as I turned back to Jarei and started reigning blows.

"That's right Era! Work that nigga! Beat his ass!" I could hear my momma hyping me up which turned me into a beast. Jarei tried to swing but me and Ju'well were all over him, not giving him room to land a solid hit. I felt someone tugging my hair and grabbed at a rough hand.

"DON'T YOU TOUCH HER!" Praylah charged Jarei's home boy, and I could only slightly see her because Jarei socked me hard on the jaw. He dazed me and I couldn't see clear but could hear my mom screaming and cursing. I even heard her gun go off and Jarei howling out in pain claiming to be shot in the foot.

. . .

"I'M fenna lay you niggas down!!!!" Jarei threw his hands up in the air and my vision became clear. Out of breath and feeling cramps all in my side, Ju'well was covering her breasts. She had grass stains all over her shirt like she had been rolling all around the front lawn. The gun went off again and this time it was Jarei's friend holding his bloody kneecap.

PRAYLAH LOOKED like she was in a zone. She football tackled Jarei down to the grass just as he was taking the time to sit up. When she got on top of him, she didn't stop swinging, I joined her along with Ju'well.

"THAT's enough girls he bloody as hell and the cops will be on the way." We slowly got off of Jarei as Ju'well landed one last kick making his front tooth fall out.

HIS EYES WERE SWOLLEN, and his was nose leaking blood. I didn't even realize all the damage we had done until it was all over. I looked at his light skin friend and he had scratches all over his neck. Praylah clawed him up badly. I couldn't believe my ears hearing him sniffle and cry lowly as he held his knee. I was surprised my mom had actually shot Jarei and his friend.

"Now I DON'T WANT to ever have to pull up again to have this conversation with you young men. Get in counseling do something to learn how to treat a woman." My mom preached. "I'll be praying for your mercy and your wounds."

. . .

MY MOM WENT to her car and sped out of the driveway and the three of us hurried and got in my car to speed back to the restaurant.

FOR THE FIRST couple of minutes, we were all breathing hard and silent until Ju'well broke that silence.

"MOMMA EARLENE WAS like Madea bouncing them tig ol' bitties! Boy, Boy, BOYYYYYA! What you doing, Boy!" We fell out laughing at Ju'well, Praylah was turning red in the face from laughing so damn hard. Ju'well even let her breast bounce up and down while sitting in the front seat imitating my momma.

"I DIDN'T KNOW ya momma was a thug like that, Era." Ju'well chuckled. I knew my mom could fight because I saw her when I was younger beat a couple of chicks up for approaching her over my no good daddy. I thought she just kept that gun to scare people but today she used that baby deuce like she was used to shooting it.

"I JUST HOPE her baby thug ass don't get in no trouble for actually shooting those two fools." I hopped on the freeway looking at the time on my radio; it showed we were running a whole hour behind. I had no clue how the restaurant was doing. I trusted my co-workers because they all did their job well. I just hoped and prayed that Debo wouldn't be there when we arrived.

. . .

71

WE ALL REMAINED quiet until we pulled into the back parking lot. A sigh escaped all of our mouths as we noticed Debo leaning against his all-white Rolls Royce truck. He switched cars so much you never knew what to expect to see him in. His dreads were pulled low into a ponytail, he rocked all white. White Gucci shirt, white jeans with all white Gucci sneakers. The nigga looked fresh and crisp with a big Cuban gold chain shining with the words Slaughter Gang in diamonds on a medallion.

"LET'S FACE THE MUSIC GIRLS." I sighed already knowing that our jobs were gone.

WE ALL GOT out of the car looking a hot mess as Debo's big gray eyes landed right on all three of us. He took us in scanning us from head to toe. Ju'well shirt was ripped so she still had to cover her breasts. The wind blew and I could feel the sting from open cuts that I hadn't realized was there.

"ALL THREE OF y'all fired. Don't go into my place of business looking like that. I will have my assistant send over your final checks. Praylah..." he paused and lowered his voice a little like she was the most delicate out of all of us which she actually was.

"GET YO' ass in the car and buckle up." Was all he said as he waited for her to pick her feet up and make her way to the car.

· · ·

72

"Thank y'all for being there for me today. It felt good to stand up for myself." She started out, ignoring the fact that she had this beastly-looking nigga blowing steam from his nose and ears behind her.

"You ain't even got to thank us. We gon' always ride, no matter how big, buff, or scary a nigga look like." I eyed Debo, hoping he got the message too. Sure, the nigga looked scary and crazy, I didn't give a damn when it came to the ones I loved. I rode for mine until the wheels fell off.

"Aye Era, you blessed that I fuck with you and you like family now. Since I'm trying to work on something serious with Praylah. Don't try to threaten a nigga like me." He turned and walked away. Praylah grabbed me then pulled Ju'well as we all shared a tight hug.

"Make sure you call me when you get home and settled." I gave Praylah a reassuring smile.

"Call us girl, I got razors and tasers for his big fine ass if he gets out of line too." Ju'well lowly spoke making us all erupt in laughter as we all walked our separate ways. A thought crossed my mind as I yelled out at my girls.

"Oh yea! Saturday night, I got y'all tickets to come to see my first-ever performance at the B.E.T. awards!" Praylah let go of the door handle to Debo's car and ran fast towards me just as Era covered her breast as she ran next in my direction.

They showered me with love and tight hugs as we all jumped up and down pumped up.

THIS IS what a real sisterhood was supposed to look like.

PRAYLAH

"*I* need to go get my daughter." I finally broke the silence not caring about Michael's attitude.

"You not getting her right now. You coming to my house so we can have a talk." He didn't look at me; just kept his focus on the road. My adrenaline was still pumping through me, and he added to that by firing me.

"Why would I come to your house When you just fuckin' fired me!" My voice elevated as I kept my eyes glued to his side profile. Ignoring the fact that he smelled good and looked even better. I was ready to do nothing else but stand up for myself. Fear crept into my bones as he cut a car to the right off and then pulled over to the side of the road hitting his hazards. Those wild gray eyes pierced my ass as he gave me an icy glare.

"Watch yo' tone with me Pray. I ain't shit like that pussy ass nigga you used of dealing with." His jaw clenched.

"I don't have to watch shit, I said I want to go get my daughter nigga!" I snapped my neck and looked at him like he was the crazy one. When he laughed it made me even more angry.

"I don't want to be around a nigga that fired me." I spat, getting pissed that he had the nerve to actually fire me. I didn't know exactly what I was mad at, but I was pissed.

"Oh... you ain't ditzy no more. You a strong black woman on ya independent shit cause you did some hood rat shit out in the streets fighting." He licked his thick cinnamon lips and chuckled. Digging in his ashtray he pulled a blunt out and sparked it, blowing smoke in my face.

"I stood up for myself, I'm not always going to be some weak female," I argued because I saw nothing wrong with my actions.

"Stood up for yourself? When you got a nigga like me ready to catch a murder charge behind a nigga even talking to you the wrong way? You want to stand up for yourself the wrong way and that's the problem, which still proves to me that you a ditzy ass broad. You want me to take you to your parent's house to go get my daughter and you look stupid as fuck. Scratches all on yo' neck; clothes looking disheveled. Man, I swear bitches is just..." I slapped him hard across his face then went to smack him again. He caught my wrist and twisted it so hard tears immediately fell as I begged him to release my hand.

The look in his eyes scared me and it seemed like he was transforming into someone else before my eyes.

"Bitch if you ever put your hands on me again, I will force myself to fall out of love with yo' slow ass and kill you!" I stopped breathing for a couple of seconds and just looked at him. This wasn't Michael, this had to be Debo.

"You like fucking with my got damn head. You know I love you for whatever fuckin' reason. Always making my heart do that itchy shit, making me second guess myself cause I know this shit ain't fuckin' normal! Now Matthew Michael Brownston does all that easy going sophisticated shit, but

Debo! You looking right at Debo nice to fucking meet you. I don't hit bitches, but I kill them for trying to do me dirty like I should have done that bitch Lakendra. Don't trigger the killer and me. Keep yo' monkey ass hands off of me!" He roared. I quickly blinked back my tears and tried to think of the next thing to do but couldn't as he zoomed out into ongoing traffic like it didn't faze him that cars were now honking at him.

He switched lanes and drove with so much aggression that I started pleading for him to slow down. I even apologized for slapping him. He ignored me and mumbled all kinds of crazy things to himself.

"Got me looking like a pussy ass nigga. That nigga still breathing after he tried to kill my bitch!" He tapped his forehead with his free hand. It dawned on me that he was triggered by me hitting him. I could see him battling hard with himself as his eyes stayed locked on the road. It dawned on me that Debo was in love with me, but Michael wanted to do things the right way and give me the proper space and time I needed to heal.

Debo's aggression made him sexy, but Michael's caring side had me wanting to know more about him. He was showing me red flags like Jarei but at the same time deep down, I knew that he would never treat or do me how Jarei did me.

"Debo!" I yelled as he got so close behind a car that it would have been a fender bender.

"What!" He took his eyes off the road and looked over at me.

"Calm down. I'm willing to go wherever you taking me, that way I can get cleaned up. Let's go to your place first so you can take your medicine since we both agreed to both take our meds and talk to Dr. Scott whenever we start feeling like we are not being ourselves." I talked carefully hoping to get through to him.

"We were going to my place anyway. I'll take that stupid ass medicine although I prefer to eat that pussy to medicate myself. You gone get cleaned up and then we go get my daughter?" He said, daughter like it was a question. Like he was waiting for me to reassure him that Heaven was his and Jarei was a thing of the past. It didn't work that way but for now I would agree.

"Yes, baby," I said softly. His eyes softened a little as we both remained quiet finishing the ride to his house. I wasn't sure what I had got myself into, but it seemed like this was how it was supposed to go at the moment. Looking over at Michael's shoulders relaxed, it felt like I calmed him down.

We got to his house, and he was back quiet, he opened the door and led me up to the second floor where I entered his massive bedroom. I didn't know what to expect but it wasn't this. His mother had to come in and decorate it because everything was neat, and it fit him. His walls were painted tan, his room was very cold, and the proof was the two ceiling fans that spun rapidly from his ceiling. Going into his bathroom I heard him cut the shower water on.

Next, I heard him opening and slamming shut his medicine cabinets. He walked back into the room with two medicine bottles. Piercing me with a pensive look.

"I'm not as bad as my dad." I tilted my head a little trying to understand what he was getting at. "I'm sorry if I scared you. I don't want you to run from me. I know that shit I said was foul, but you triggered the fuck out of me hitting me like I was some random nigga off the streets." He placed the pill bottles on his cherry wood dresser and opened up the tops to both bottles. I watched him intently take two pills with no water. I even heard him crunching on them like it was candy.

78

"Why not use water?" I asked really wanting to know.

"My dad… whenever he used to have manic episodes he would chew his pills and I guess it helped that shit work faster." He shrugged and took another.

"Stop doing that, it doesn't make the pills work faster Michael. You can overdose and send your body into shock that way. It's called dose dumping. Look, how bout we get in the shower together and relax ourselves." I surprised myself at what I was suggesting. He seemed antsy and still on edge.

"You tryna feel me up, when I'm still mad at you sugar mommy." He smirked and walked up to me grabbing a hand full of my ass. I blushed hard and didn't fight to remove his hands from my backside. I enjoyed the closeness and intimacy that he offered me whenever he did offer it. Michael constantly made me feel like a prized possession. When he stared at me, he made me feel like I was the sexiest woman alive.

"No, I'm just trying to calm your nerves since I triggered them. We both were wrong today. I was wrong for slapping you and you were wrong for firing me and my friends then calling me a bitch." I made sure to add him firing me in the equation.

"Nah, y'all staying fired. I have to run a successful business and I don't like exposing who I am. Today I had to do that shit because my manager and the rest of y'all ran off the job stealing companies time by not clocking out just to go fight a lame ass nigga that I could've killed weeks ago."

"Why do you want to kill your friend?" I asked curiously.

"For multiple reasons now. The first was that he owed me money, even though he paid up I don't give no man walking a pass for being late. Second, I found out that he was your baby daddy, and I don't like that cause you my woman and he violated you knowing that you just needed help and guidance to get back on the right path with your bipolar and depression. Praylah, you my sugar mommy now. You sweet, soft and sexy as fuck. The first time I laid eyes on you something inside of me rather it was crazy or sane said that we were meant to be. You a delicate flower, a woman. You shouldn't be treated the way that nigga has treated you. So now I got to prove and show you some shit you ain't never been shown." He kissed my neck then trailed his tongue up to my chin and sucked on it softly then ended it with a peck.

"A nigga might not be a hundred percent fit for this shit, but you start renovating my heart the moment you opened your mouth and start spitting that ditzy shit." He captured my lips and kissed me as I pushed him back playfully with his solid chest.

"Go rinse your mouth, Michael." I giggled but was still serious.

"You got me tasting those nasty pills you chewed up, crazy man."

"Alright come on stinky butt, let's shower." He slapped me hard on the ass making it ripple and shake as I yelped out loud. Rubbing the sting out, I followed him to the shower feeling better about everything. Maybe Michael was renovating my heart as well because each time I found myself next to him, the pain and betrayal from Jarei left my mind.

DEBO

"*D*id you say something Michael?" I snapped my head in Praylah's direction enjoying the view of her sexy ass being laid up in my king size bed. It was nearing seven in the evening. Although I was anxious to meet who I now considered my daughter. Praylah seemed okay with Heaven staying at her parents' house. To be real, I was ready to get all the formalities out the way. I already had her parents' address and when I knew that Praylah had Heaven and they were settled, I planned on paying Praylah's parents a visit.

They probably didn't know what was what. Praylah seemed like the type to take pride and whatever her parents thought of her, and I couldn't do shit but respect that. I puffed on my blunt as all kinds of thoughts roamed my head. Praylah was my sanity, her being so close to me gave me a peace that I never knew I needed. She came with some shit just like I did. We both were probably crazy as hell but our crazy fit each other well in my head. I just had to keep reminding myself to pace it all and take my time.

Earlier when I flipped the fuck out, it was like that voice

81

in my head took over and I had no other choice but to sit back and watch it take control. It felt like I had been watching a damn movie, praying that nothing bad happened while wishing I could intervene. That voice and I feared losing Praylah. What's crazy is before her, I never felt so anxious to take my meds because I felt my behavior was okay. My intrusive thoughts and my evil ways were what I felt like I needed, especially being in the streets and running shit tough. I didn't need a conscious when I went out to kill and fuck shit up.

With Praylah, I wanted my conscious intact, I wanted to treat her good. I just never wanted her to mistake me as a pussy ass nigga since I was being kind and so fuckin' smitten with her. Her slapping me was a big no go, I didn't put my hands on women and women knew better then to try to test me like Praylah did earlier by putting her hands on me.

"Nah, I ain't said shit but you better never put your hands on me again. No matter how mad you get... don't ever put your hands on me again Pray. I'll never try to hurt you physically and as far as emotionally... I'll do my very best." I let my eyes roam her curvy thick body, we locked eyes for a while before she smiled and giggled.

"Why you always so serious? Everything you say seems to have a deep meaning." She sat up, I wanted to have her take my white tee off so I could see those pretty melons. My mind went right to nasty thoughts as I eyed her hardened nipples that was playing peekaboo with my vision.

"Cause I'm a serious ass nigga." I shrugged and got up off the bed.

"Come on, I got some steak, potatoes, and shit in the kitchen that I want you to whip up for us. I need to make sure you can really cook since you gon' be my wife one day. I don't like buying out to eat if it's not from my restaurant. Cooking is something that I will do most of the time, but it would be a plus if my woman knows how to cook as well." She batted her eyes and remained expressionless. I hoped like hell she could cook.

Especially since she had a kid, I hated it when I saw parents buying their kids fast food like McDonald's and all that other unhealthy bullshit. Anything I cooked in my kitchen was made from scratch, thanks to my mom and dad for teaching a nigga that. I just really fell in love with creating and making bomb ass meals. On my down time, I created new shit for my franchise menus.

"What if I don't know how to cook? Is that a deal breaker for you?" She asked nervously and that shit had me smiling hard as fuck. I liked the fact that she cared about how I would feel about her not being able to cook. I also was glad that she seemed to be getting it through her head that we both was feeling the fuck out of each other and soon we would become something more when she got over that bitch ass nigga Sosa and let me kill him without trying to run far away from me.

"I'll teach you if you don't know, and, if I ever get too busy, I'll put you through classes to learn." I pulled her close and placed my hands underneath her heavy ass cheeks. I was an ass man; I loved a woman with a heavy ass booty.

"That's sweet of you Michael." She pecked me on the nose like I was a bitch and I frowned at her silly ass and paused.

"Don't ever do no feminine shit like that to me again man." I shook my head and led her out the room to my big ass kitchen. One of my favorite places in my house. Looking at my spacious countertops and all the room I had to play around with Praylah. I made a mental note that when I test tasted the food she prepared, I was gon' toss her ass on the counters and eat her first then have her make me a big plate of her cooking.

"You already make me nervous, go do something while I prepare this grand dinner you want." She smirked and I just stood there probably creeping her out. What Praylah didn't understand was I liked just staring at her light bright ass. Her facial features down to her round face and curly lashes was perfect as fuck to me. I loved all the weight she carried and how fluffy and soft she was. The smell of her without perfume was a special smell that only she had.

I walked down my long hallways trying to figure out what there was I could do to kill time. Usually, I'd be out in the streets scaring niggas to death but since I didn't want to let Praylah's unpredictable ass out of my eyesight I had no other choice but to sit idle and I liked it.

Alesia, my assistant, crossed my mind just as I walked into my man cave where I kept all my weed and top shelf liquor. I dialed Alesia number and placed the phone on speaker, sitting it on my bar top. The phone rang three times then the voicemail picked up, causing me to put my bottle of Moet Cliché down. Yea, a nigga was drinking something light and sexy. I didn't want to be off hard liquor while chilling with my sugar mommy.

I could feel the deep crease forming in the center of my forehead. Alesia was supposed to be available to me twenty-four seven around the clock. It's the main reason why I paid her a hefty salary and sent her six figure tips to keep her happy although I stressed her ass to the max. I didn't really want shit from her right now but to see what it was that I needed to catch up on. Which meetings she recorded for me with her and my team making new deals that I would need to look over to make sure it was a go with my final say so.

I desperately needed to make a decision when it came to my legal shit and street shit. I loved the streets a lot, it was my first love, but I was starting to fall out of love with that shit. I was ready to settle down and be about some other shit that had no risk of getting caught up in a grave or jail cell. I highly doubted any of the two because our organization had people in higher places in our back pockets.

I was too curious on why Alesia ignored my call. She always answered even when she was in bed. Hell, one time I think she answered in the middle of getting laid. I applauded her for that shit because Alesia always put business first, something I was working on. Popping the bottle, I tilted my glass to the side and poured up a glass of Moet. I down the first glass then poured a second and decided to call Alesia again, this time she answered on the first ring. *Good girl*, I thought.

"Hey Mrrrrrr. Mich, Brownstown." She giggled then caught herself from laughing. I couldn't hold back my own smile because Alesia was buzzed up and feeling good, still trying to remain professional.

"What you got up?" I decided to make small talk. I never really got personal with anyone that worked with me besides Praylah, it was bad for business. Over the years though, Alesia and I were considered good business partners even though her position was considered my assistant, she helped me in many ways going above and beyond her actual position.

"I'm out at a hookah lounge with my cousin Kandy. Did you need anything, I have my iPad and laptop in my purse."

"Nah, you good. Just call me early morning and let me know what I need to catch up on and be safe. No more drinks for you Alesia and make sure you get a driver." I hung up. Picking up the bottle of Moet, I left the glass cup on the bar top and grabbed my phone and went to sit in my lounge chair that had my weed box on top of a small desk that connected to the chair. A gift from my mom. I broke down my weed and twisted it up and just sat in silence feeling good to be actually home.

I was sitting here, ready to get up and go see what Praylah was doing. I didn't know what the fuck to do with myself. Looking at my phone, I sparked my blunt and decided to facetime Honor. I didn't do the facetime shit, so I was prepared for her to start talking shit and clowning a nigga.

"Yo' what the fuck? Nigga facetime yo' girl not me." She cheesed into the phone like she was happy to see me. It did feel different video calling her instead of calling her regular. I could see Ju'well standing behind her and nodded my head at her. Ju'well and Honor was a good look. I could tell that my homie was really happy with ol' girl. Ju'well rolled her eyes hard at me and I remembered that I had fired her feisty ass.

"Ain't no hard feelings baby girl. Be more professional next time." I schooled her and she walked off.

"That was fucked up you fired my girl nigga." Honor looked into the phone and shook her head at me. I sat the phone against my bottle of Moet to hold it up and shrugged my big shoulders. The three of those girls pissed me off.

"Nah, they was wrong. Had me exposing who the fuck I was. Leaving work to go whoop a nigga ass, a nigga that Pray should've let me kill." I clenched my jaws getting pissed all over again. Praylah really didn't know how stupid she had moved. Anything could've happened while she called herself growing balls. Besides, I didn't want my girl apart of fighting and handling niggas when that was my job.

"Yea, I want that piece and that small ring over there." Ju'well sat the phone down and I saw a black ceiling and already knew where the hell she was at. Looking at the time, and noting that it was nearing nine pm. I knew she had met at our private jeweler place. We spent good money with Johny Boy, and he would only open after hours to appease us.

"Look at you, big ass trick. Already tricking on a broad." I pestered with Honor because she was the main one preaching to niggas about not loving these hoes.

"Nigga me? Look at you! Paid apartments, foreign cars... you probably bout to wire me some money right now since I'm right here next to Johny boy." She giggled and a thought crossed my head.

"You damn right, I'm bout to wire you a hundred and fifty bands now. Ask Johny Boy if he got some pink diamonds? I want Praylah to have a pink diamond ring on her toes and finger." I stopped talking and thought for a second.

"Pink diamond bracelet and necklace too. Tell him to make a ring and necklace, plus earrings for my daughter. If he need sizes ask ya girl Ju'well since that's her homegirl." I chuckled watching Honor's caramel face turn red as her high ass cheek bones damn near touched her chinky ass eyes.

"Oh shit, next is a wedding ring!" She looked excited as hell, and I just shook my head because I wasn't on marriage just yet. Shit, my feelings were moving fast as hell for Praylah and didn't really know how to feel about that.

"Nigga stop with all that. Just get the shit and drop it off to my house." I ended the call. I didn't really feel too comfortable expressing how I felt about Praylah. Lakendra was calling, and I quickly ignored her call. There was no point in me blocking the bitch because all she would end up doing is calling from another number or one of those annoying ass apps.

I always imagined me and Lakendra being good ass friends beside me falling out of love with her. I still had love for her dog ass but as time went on that love was starting to vanish. If she kept being such a nuisance, I would get rid of her with quickness. I smoked two more blunts until I felt good and higher than the clouds.

Deciding to mess with my red head, I left everything in the room and walked out. Soon as I exited the room, the smell of whatever Praylah was cooking hit my nose. I didn't have to taste it to know it was good. The smell alone told me just that.

My dick start bricking up at the thought of Praylah really knowing how to cook. I was a big hungry nigga so a woman knowing how to cook was something that I could fuck with. I thought I was making the shit a little easy for her, giving her a steak to cook. I even sat out instant mashed potatoes to test her cooking skills. If she did make a nigga instant mashed potatoes, then I wouldn't eat it but would try the steak.

Bending the corner, I eased into the kitchen quietly and just watched Praylah's back. My eyes scanned her backside from that big head of hers down to her heart shaped wide ass booty. Praylah's was in her own little world humming and mashing some shit in a pot. I already knew it was potatoes, that shit had me smiling hard as hell. She was smart, she didn't dare make a nigga no instant mashed potatoes.

I crept up on her and leaned down to kiss the nape of her neck. She shivered a little then turned around to face me. Innocent eyes staring right into my wild orbs. Looking in Praylah's eyes made me feel a way. Like I had to protect her by all means necessary. A crazy thought crossed my mind and I tried to ignore and drop it.

As my hard dick landed on her soft stomach and I held her by the bottom of her ass cheeks. My next step was plotting a way to get her to move in with me. That shit wasn't happening any time soon, so I didn't want to bring that up to her and have her looking at me funny.

"You walked right past your plate. I decided to make two pots of mashed potatoes only because I like adding garlic and extra sour cream to mine before I mash all the other ingredients together. So, the potatoes on your plate along with your smothered steak is traditional." Every time she talked to me; she talked like she was a little guarded.

Every now and then Pray would get real bold and sassy. I wanted her confidant all the time. When she got nervous about something, she had a hard time making eye contact. Her eyes would land on me for seconds then look at everything else surrounding us.

I released her ass and walked to the kitchen island. Picking up my plate, everything on it looked good.

"I want you to put some of your special mash potatoes on my plate next to the traditional ones." She nodded her head and took the plate, adding a nice amount. When she got done, I told her to make a plate and then we headed towards my dining room. I took a seat while Praylah went to get us something to drink. Soon as I cut into my smothered steak and put it inside of my mouth, I instantly fell in love.

I followed up with her special mashed potatoes then tasted the traditional ones. They both tasted like she added her personal touch to them. Shit was so good it had me excited as fuck to see what else she could cook. Growing up, one thing I looked forward to was a homecooked tasty meal. That shit made me fall in love with food. I loved Deserts and all of that good shit. My momma had me spoiled so when I grew up, I started teaching myself how to cook.

By the time Praylah sat down to eat her food, my plate was halfway gone. I looked at her intently as she savored every bite that she took. She licked her lips each time she placed food into her mouth.

"Why are you looking at me like that Michael?" she picked up a napkin and gently dapped around her mouth to make sure she didn't have food on her mouth. Women cared about shit like that. I didn't give a fuck if she had the shit dripping down her chest. Her cooking was just that good.

"I want to taste you, like your cooking, Pray. Then... I want to stick my dick all the way inside of you and fuck you hard then slow as fuck. If you don't feel comfortable with that then it's cool. I'll just go shower and beat the fuck out of my dick thinking about how well you fed a nigga." Silence. That was too be expected, Praylah had to understand that I was direct as fuck, and she had a nigga obsessed with everything there was about her.

"You can, only if you make me feel pain and pleasure." Her eyes lowered, it's like she was seducing me with her orbs.

"Praylah, baby... I only want to let you feel pain and pleasure when you're mentally stable. I don't want to enhance any of your negative feelings are thoughts." When Praylah told me that she sometimes welcomed that bitch ass nigga Sosa hitting her to snap her back into reality because she liked pain when she was depressed. That shit made me think hard, I wasn't going into this new situation with her applying pain in her life even though it would make her feel good.

Nothing from me would hurt, shit I planned on fucking her hard then slow. I just didn't want her to start thinking that I would really make some shit hurt. It was only a metaphor when I said I'll make some shit painfully good.

"When I'm around you Michael, I feel good. I'm not in a bad space right now. Even though I begged my friends not to go mess with Jarei. I'll admit that it felt good to cause him pain instead of it being the other way around. I meant what I said to you a couple of seconds ago in a different way. I just want to feel you because you make me feel special. You make me disagree with the fucked up and negative thoughts that I have about myself. I don't want to rush anything… but then again, I don't want what we have going to stop."

What I admire right now was Praylah maintaining eye contact with me. Pushing my plate to the side. I stood up and dropped my boxers and sat right back down.

"Come here, sugar mommy." I stared at her with so much hunger like I was ready to devour her thick ass. "Take all that shit off along the way then come sit on this table." She was nervous. Her eyes got skittish again looking at everything around us except for keeping them pretty big orbs on me.

"You were bold and talking straight to me a few seconds ago. Keep that same energy Praylah. Keep yo' eyes on me and take those muthafuckin' clothes off." I pulled my bottom lip in with my top row of teeth. When she got all of her clothes off and was standing in front of me, I pulled her between my legs and caressed the sides of her arms then moved my right hand down the middle of her plump breast down to her stomach.

Inhaling her scent, I kissed her stomach and then stuck my tongue inside of her navel. She gasped hard then held her breath. I kissed and bit all over her pudgy stomach. Every couple of seconds my eyes landed on her fat mound that sat underneath her stomach peeking out. I looked into her eyes grabbing a handful of ass and smacking it.

"You so fucking sexy, Pray. So fucking thick and beautiful." I stood up and picked her off her feet. Sitting her at the edge of my dining room table. I took a seat and pulled my chair close until I was face to face with her pretty ass pussy.

"What you want me to do sugar mommy? You dripping like hell ma." My stomach growled even though I just ate, she had me starving to taste her.

"I want you to eat me until you full." She kept eye contact; I used my hand to open up her sex. Blowing on it like it was too hot to touch, I dipped my tongue in and circled her erect clit with my tongue then enclosed my entire mouth around her sweet pearl.

"Oh, my goodness Michael!" She leaned back on her elbows, and when she did that her pussy was more in my face, even better.

"Feed this pussy to me Praylah." I grabbed her hips then dragged my tongue to her snug tunnel. Dipping my tongue in and out of her, I let my nose gently massage her clit. Her hips kept thrusting forward like she was fucking my tongue.

"Grab those pretty titties baby and pinch those nipples." I made my voice clear as I continued my assault. "Fuck you taste so fucking sweet, stinky girl." I sat up a little and eyed her swollen lips. using three fingers, I tapped her pussy with my fingers, enjoying the wet sound it made then dipped my head back in attacking her sex.

Keeping my mouth on her center, I watched her sexy ass do exactly what I told her and that shit really had me thrilled.

"I'm about to wait... Mi! Oh shit!" She screeched trying to clamp her thighs shut but my face was stopping her from doing so. Her pussy bucked all in my mouth as I held her sex captive sucking every drip of wetness she had. When I came up for air, Praylah's pussy was glistening wet. My dick was so hard it ached. Praylah was sprawled out on her back taking deep breaths.

I wasn't giving her a chance to recover. I stood and aligned my dick with her sex and entered her slowly. Her pussy sucked me in, making my toes curl like a bitch.

"Pray?" I grunted deep inside of her as I started beating it up.

"Yes daddy?" She cooed, locking eyes with me.

"You fucking me up in the head sugar mommy." I

grabbed her waist and slid her sexy ass back and forth on my dick.

"I'll give you anything you want baby. Tell daddy what you want." I pleaded with her with my eyes.

Watching her titties bounce with each stroke had me in a trance.

"Give us our jobs back." She flexed and contracted her pussy muscles on a nigga and had my mind gone.

"You got that baby." I grunted and growled trying to keep from moaning. I really thought about what she had asked and chuckled lowly. Praylah thought she was slick, and I had to give it to her. No sane man would be able to tell her ass no while being deep inside of this gushy shit.

"Promise me, baby." Fuck she was sending me.

"I promise Pray, fuck! Unchoke my dick baby and let a nigga stroke this shit. You tryna make me nut." I bit into my bottom lip as she relaxed her walls on the shaft of my dick. I noticed her stomach cave in, her eyes rolled back. That pussy gripped my damn dick like it was trying to keep my shit forever.

This was the kind of pussy that a nigga had to praise and take care of. Sosa bitch ass just ain't know what the fuck he was doing with this shit. Praylah's pussy had me ready to annihilate any nigga who even had thoughts or wants to smash her. Praylah belonged to me, I didn't give a fuck how slow she wanted to take shit. This was the kind of pussy that could dominate and tame a beast ass nigga like myself.

Her eyes flickered open, and I suddenly had the urge to feel her close to me. Making her wrap her thick warm thighs around my waist I pulled her close against my chest.

"You got my fuckin' mind girl." I talked directly in her ear and listened to her whimper. Using the bottom of her ass I pushed her up and down my dick. Needing full access to the pussy I placed each leg in my arms and widened my stance by spreading my feet apart. I squatted with her legs locked in each arm and went to work on her sex. Her head was tilted back, mouth wide open as I captured her neck with my teeth and bit down gently.

"I'm cumming again Baby!" She screamed and sat up to grab my shoulders as I kissed her feverishly.

"Nut all on this dick baby." And like a good fucking girl she rained down all on me. Leaving the dining area, I carried her up the steps and put her pretty ass into too many positions to remember. At the end of all the heavy fucking, I blew on her swollen red pussy lips and kissed the pain away until she drifted off to sleep.

I puffed on a fat ass back wood and just stared down at Praylah. She had a white towel tucked between her legs and was snoring lightly.

"My sugar fucking mommy. I hope she knew that she had a niggas heart, and she was slowly starting to capture my soul.

ERA

I swear, life always had a way of throwing curve balls. I felt like I had done a horrible job at my performance but based on the blogs they were loving it. It seemed like the bad comments on my performance were sticking out more than the thousands of good comments. During my second song, my stomach felt like someone had taken a knife and dragged it across, busting my guts open. I thought maybe my period which had been missing for weeks now was making its appearance but that wasn't the case at all.

Sweat gathered on my forehead towards the end of my song and I started to feel super lightheaded. In my mind, the song that I was singing sounded like a bunch of jumble. I cried at the standing ovation, said my thanks, and hurried off the stage to throw everything that I had inside of my stomach.

I was now on the bathroom floor of my fitting room crying my heart out because I didn't understand what was going on with my body. For the past couple of weeks, I had these spells of feeling sick and not really wanting to do much. I pushed myself hard because I didn't have any time to waste when it came to my career.

"It seems to me like its pregnancy symptoms chile." Shelby leaned against the door frame staring down at me. I quickly shook my head no and then stood up.

"It can't be that though, well I don't think it is." My mind went back to the night that me and Soulful spent together. Fear struck me like lightning. We were so reckless that night, not using any protection. The thought of me being pregnant by him and how the blogs would eat me alive for sleeping with a married man had me falling down and hugging the toilet again.

"Yea, definitely pregnant symptoms. Take it from a woman that has two grown kids. Sometimes the first trimester doesn't seem to hit as hard for some. A lot of women though can get really sick in the beginning." She gave me a sympathetic look and my stomach felt queasy again.

"What should I do?" I looked at her like she was my savor.

"I don't believe in abortion but as your manager if that's something you would like to do. I can get you in somewhere undetected, without the media getting a hold of what it is you are doing." She stopped talking like she was thinking of something else.

"If you are pregnant, then I feel like the right thing for you to do is talk to who the father is." That's the part I didn't want to hear.

"I'm scared Shelby. This is my career, how am I supposed to navigate through this?" A lone tear fell down my chubby cheek. I couldn't believe how careless I was that night.

"You will navigate through it, with me right by your side. You know how many women came into the industry pregnant and still made a big name for themselves? You will release music, become big, and still have time to be a nurturing mother. Even if I got to take turns and feed the baby." She giggled and I joined her, still afraid of the outcome of all of this. I didn't want Soulful thinking that I was just some typical hood rat. Fucking niggas on the first night then trying to trap him because of who he was.

What I wouldn't do is get rid of my baby. I just couldn't see myself killing something so precious and innocent. My mom always said that I was a gift from God. Just the mere thought of this high possibility of being pregnant had me silently thanking God for sending me this gift, even if it came unexpected. The circumstances had me scared shitless but just like any other obstacle I was ready to face whatever this was.

"Girl first let me help you up off this nasty floor in that expensive ass gown. We still have to celebrate your success tonight." I stood on wobbly legs from dropping down so hard to the tile floor. Giving her a weak smile, I wanted so bad to cancel tonight's festivities. I just didn't want to let Praylah down. She was so excited since she got us our jobs back. She even convinced Debo to let her throw a small get-together at his restaurant after hours.

I nicely declined on getting my job back since I really needed to focus on my thriving music career.

"Cheer up, we have to celebrate. You are viral and what matters the most is you're not going viral from doing some stupid prank on the internet. You're viral because the world loves your raw and uncut talent. Era, you are authentic and beautiful, and people can feel all the good vibes and energies that radiate off of you." Shelby had my grown ass blushing. Besides me getting sick, it felt good having my family and friends in that audience tonight.

Big-time celebrities sat in that audience clapping for me. Not only that, but Devin's bitch ass was there with the bitch I caught him fucking at the studio. It's like soon as I hit that stage, me and him locked eyes and it was like he saw a ghost. I love it when a person counts me out. I looked beautiful and like Shelby said, no one really noticed me getting sick towards the end.

The adrenaline that I felt from it all was just too much and I really couldn't believe that my dreams were finally coming true. One thing that I would never lose sight of was myself and remaining humble and giving all my praises to God. Devin tried to break me and take the one thing that I cherished away and that was my dream.

I stayed in my dressing room cleaning myself up and changing out of my expensive gown. I brought my duffle bag to put on my white ripped up jeans that hugged every curve that I had to offer. I was feeling sexy and confident, so I put on my MCM crop top shirt. I paired it with the monogram MCM belt and hat. Looking down at my feet I smirked at my fresh MCM sneakers to match. I looked good as hell and just prayed that my stomach didn't cut up again on me.

I walked out of the bathroom area to let Shelby know that I was ready to leave. Stopping right outside the bathroom door my eyes landed on Devin. Shelby gave him the look of death, crossing her arms across her chest.

"We really need to talk Era, alone." Looking over at Shelby I nodded my head to give her the okay. I didn't fear Devin, I just couldn't stand his ass.

"The button for security is right on your vanity. I'll be in the next room calling our driver for the night." Shelby walked out and I took a seat on the small leather sofa.

"How can I help you, Devin?" He licked his lips as he grabbed the stool from the vanity that I used before my show. He placed the stool a couple of inches away from me and took a seat on it. Devin was beyond handsome. Those green, emerald eyes twinkled as he stared into my eyes giving me the puppy dog look. I already knew that he was getting ready to beg for his position back in my life. I was a little too excited to turn his ass down.

He gave me his panty wetting smile and licked those pink lips of his to lubricate all the lies that was about to spill from his dumb ass mouth.

"I miss the fuck out of you Era and I'm so proud of you Ma." If I was a weak bitch, then his fine ass would have really got to me. All I could do right now was feel sorry for the next bitch that had to sit up and be charmed by his conniving ass.

"Thank you, Devin. I appreciate you. If that's all, I need to be leaving for my party." I stood and he quickly followed suit. Stepping into my personal space, he placed his hands on my wide hips and pulled me close.

"Come on, Era. You didn't hear me just say I miss you baby? You the only woman that was really holding a nigga down and being there for me. I fucked up one time, you got to forgive me." He lowered his lips onto my neck and kissed softly sending tremors down my spine. Some male attention did feel good, it felt so good that I let him grab a handful of my pear-shaped ass and squeeze tight.

Whimpering a little, I cleared my thoughts and placed my hands on his shoulders to create some space.

"Devin, I don't want to sound like some broken record. You hurt me, and you're only sorry because you got caught. Instead of you owning up and being remorseful, you shitted on me. You brought a whole contract to my house, a contract that could have changed my life. I stayed up late nights talking to you about my dreams and how much I love to sing. You shitted on me right after you broke my heart. I can't forgive you for that shit." He didn't say anything, so I continued.

99

"You were happy here tonight with the girl I caught you fucking. You weren't expecting to see me on that stage doing what you tried to take away from me. I still love you; I just can't rock with you." He started to chuckle. Fire was dancing in his green eyes like he was angry, and I prepared myself for him to say so fucked up shit.

"Come on now Era... Be for real right now. Look at you, I mean you pretty and chocolate but you big as fuck. I'm actually a good look for you, I compliment you well. You think cause Shelby out here giving you pitiful handouts that you gone get far. You sneaking around probably reaching out to my industry friends to get an expensive bitch like Shelby on your team. You know the money will run out. What? You back working like a slave smelling like greasy ass food at that restaurant? Or.... Is you giving that good ass pussy away to make a nigga trick cause I know you-" I raised my hand and slapped the fuck out of Devin.

"I love when people reveal exactly how they been feeling. Don't worry about what I'm doing and how the fuck I'm doing that shit. Just be prepared to be sick of hearing and seeing me around this industry." I walked away as he shouted and called me all kinds of fat bitches. Picking up my duffle bag, security was waiting right outside my door. Handing him my bag I knocked at Shelby door with no ill feelings.

Niggas like Devin were the worse. If I was a weak-ass bitch, I would've taken him back then let him play me again.

SOULFUL HURTZ

"*D*on't tell me shit about loyalty when you couldn't even show me that shit!" I yelled at the top of my lungs feeling weak and defeated. My team lost the Superbowl, and I felt like I let them down. My head wasn't in the game trying to finalize my divorce with Jocelyn. She tried to do everything in her power to save our marriage like offering to get help for her drug habit.

"I WENT and got an abortion Soulful! There was no point in keeping that baby if it breaks us apart. Soulful listen to me... after losing my brother, I just found myself trying to numb all the pain from that. I tried the drugs and couldn't stop. I start feeling jealous of you. I don't know exactly why. It just felt like I had to share my husband with the NFL! You were never really here and when you were here it was all about your sisters."

.   .   .

THE TEARS that decorated her face should have moved me and made me feel sorry for her, but it didn't do any of that. All I heard was a bunch of excuses for the bullshit she had done. I would've made us work beyond all the long-term cheating she did. The fact that she was pregnant by this nigga showed me how much out of love she was with me. Shit crushed me to my core.

ANOTHER THING WAS, I didn't want to deal with a drug user. It's like once a person got hooked on drugs, they had the possibility of relapsing. Not saying Jocelyn could beat the drugs and never go back to them. I just didn't want to chance that shit. I went through enough disappointment dealing with my mom. All the fake getting clean talks and my mom telling me that she would do better. Promising not only me but my little sisters then doing nothing but disappointing us all.

"WHY WOULD I put myself through more bullshit with you Jah? Like really tell a nigga why the fuck should I give us a chance? Our divorce is final. Will I be there for you? Yes, I will when I really don't even have to do that. As far as us as a union, I can't do it. I don't even look at you the same man. You making this shit hard."

"I'm not going anywhere Soulful. I love you too much." She stood off the bed and eyed me somberly. I couldn't even believe what I was looking at. Jocelyn looked pitiful, desperate, and weak. I didn't want to kick her while she was down, but I needed her to understand that shit with us became dead from the moment she admitted to being pregnant by another nigga.

. . .

I HAD time to think about all of her actions. Jocelyn would become my downfall if I decided to stay with her. She already had me making calls and getting niggas killed because I felt violated. When I really thought deeply about all of this shit, I knew deep down I would never forgive Jah for cheating on me. After all the years of being faithful, something drove me to cheat. I wasn't some cheating ass nigga but after all this time I became one and just one night and couldn't seem to get the black thick beauty out of my mental.

"DID you hear what I said Soulful?" Her voice cracked as I looked into her dry tear-stricken face.

"YEA, I heard you. I just don't understand you still. You don't got to go nowhere Jah. This house is yours and paid for. I would turn it over so it could be fully in your name, but I can't trust you on that. You might sell the house and go buy the shit I use to sell to survive." She dramatically fell down to her knees and cried out loud and hard. I felt numb inside so none of it moved me.

"I'M GIVING you an allowance of ten thousand dollars a month. You will be drugged test, so rather you get clean or not it's up to you. The cars and all that nice shit stays here, it's yours. The only thing that I will be taking is my new Range Rover, my clothes and jewelry. If your drug test comes back negative and shit in the house come up missing when I come to check in with you. Then I will take your allowance away and treat you how I used to treat my momma." She looked up at me like she was staring at a stranger.

. . .

IT FUCKED me up that I even had to talk and treat her this way, but Jocelyn was no longer considered my wife. If I was totally heartless, I'd kick her out on the streets or kill her ass and pay the money out to make it appear as a freak accident.

"IF YOU GET BACK on drugs and I notice you selling cars and the house is fucked up then I will kick you out of here and place you back in the projects so you can be a real smoker broad. I'll change my fuckin' number and stop by the hood once a month to bring your ass groceries and shit. You know that I'm a man of my word." I warned her. She balled her pretty face up and now looked at me with hate.

"JUST GO SOULFUL, I hate I ever took you back when you left me the first time. I took on you and those girls and all your mommy issues and now you want to turn your fucking back on me." I chuckled bitterly at the audacity of this bitch. More and more I was starting to have a strong dislike for her ass.

"YEA, I know. I hate I ever even doubled back with you when I could've been just fine without yo' weak ass." I gave her my broad back and walked out carrying the last of my shit. I knew soon as I left my new crib to come here and get the last of my shit that I would have to face Jocelyn. I paid extra money just to expedite my divorce and today was all the closure that I was going to allow myself to have with Jocelyn.

. . .

SOON AS I hit the locks on my cocaine white Range Rover, Debo was calling me. Since that shit went down with Dmack, we both been talking a lot more. I was interested in starting a summer league with men from Watts, mainly the projects. My men would be facing off with his Los Angeles men better known as his Slaughter gang niggas.

"WHAT'S GOOD NIGGA?"

"SHIT MAINTAINING bout to hit a couple of corners and check up on my girl. I was calling to see when I could meet up with you, so we can put together these different game days and practice. Usually, me and my nigga Sosa throw a big annual game like the one you came to before. Now I'm trying to do some new shit. I think you will like my idea." I perked up at that. I really needed something to get my mind off of all the bullshit I had going on. Losing a Superbowl was a big thing as well.

A lot of people tried to make the shit feel better by saying at least my team made it to the Superbowl. In my eyes, I felt like what was the point of celebrating going when you indeed didn't get that ring.

"I'M FREE RIGHT NOW, if you got the time."

"BET, meet me at my restaurant. I got to meet with yo' girl to give her this last check." I looked at the phone wondering what the hell he meant by my girl. Then my mind went to Era and a silly ass smile appeared on my face.

. . .

"Bet. I'm on the way." Shit, I didn't know what Era thought of me. I know what all I thought of her. She was talented, pretty as hell and all natural. I loved her voice, that shit touched a niggas soul and her pussy felt and tasted immaculate.

* * *

I sat inside of the back of Debo's restaurant eating Hennessy wings. I kept replaying me and Jocelyn's conversation, not believing after all these years this was where we were. I had to really realize that nothing was forever. Loss is inevitable and feelings were best locked away and buried somewhere safe if a person didn't want to risk being hurt. I couldn't deny my feelings, I just didn't want to become a bitter ass nigga which was why I felt like I should still provide for Jah.

Looking up towards the restaurant entrance my eyes landed on Era. My stomach rumbled like I was hungry when I've already stuffed myself with over ten wings and garlic fries. It's obvious she's not here for work. She's wearing a black halter romper with some Rick Owen boots. My eyes roam her full figure, dick stiffening watching her hips sway to a silent beat. We connect eyes and she stops walking momentarily as I hold my hand up to signal her sexy ass over to my table.

She seemed reluctant, pushing her purse more up on her shoulders. Era started my way and had me locked in with her deep set of eyes. Era was beyond beautiful, her rich chocolate skin tone looked tasty as fuck. I was anxious to smell her scent and have her close to me. The chemistry between us was strong, I couldn't deny it the first time I laid eyes on her.

ERA WALKED UP SMELLING like wild berries and soft sandalwood.

"Is your wife about to pop out on us?" She stuck her nose up with that soft ass voice of hers. Ignoring her sarcasm. I motioned for her to sit down.

"NAH, NO WIFE." I looked her in the eyes then let my eyes drop to her cleavage, breast peaking looking ripe as hell. Era clears her throat with her brows plunged downward like she is about to scold me for looking at something I just could resist.

"DON'T TELL me you're a liar as well." She chuckled like she was annoyed.

"ERA, we don't know each other, it's a lot we should know. So, hold off on all the judging and assumptions so we can exchange numbers and get fully acquainted." My words seemed to set a fire under her ass, she stood abruptly and talked in a low comical threatening tone.

. . .

"NIGGA, don't think because you sent Shelby my way, I owe you something cause I don't. You are married don't lie to me, you said that shit before you fucked me good and ran out the room talking about your wife." I smirked up at her breast first then finally gave her my eyes.

"I FUCKED YOU GOOD ERA?" I licked my bottom lip and inhaled her. Seeming caught off guard she took a couple steps back as she looked off briefly. When she looked back into my eyes, I paused for a minute noting the somber look covering her face. Those eyes slowly welled with tears.

"Yea, you fucked me so good that you impregnated me." She said that part low and walked off. The fuck? I had a right mind to chase her but for some reason I stayed planted right in my seat. My stomach tightened as a million emotions flooded me. A baby? A fucking baby? I was disappointed at the lack of responsibility I lacked when fucking Era raw. Happiness because I've been wanting a kid for years now. Fear struck me for my career because I didn't know what kind of woman Era was.

SHE SEEMED like a good ass woman with resentment towards men with the way she looked at me.

"NIGGA YOU LOOK like you just received the worse news ever." I looked up at this big ass nigga Debo and shook my head. Soon as he took a seat a waitress appeared in seconds.

. . .

"GET PRAYLAH TO SERVE ME." He didn't even bother looking up at the blonde head that appeared perky and eager to serve him.

"NIGGA ERA just told me I got her pregnant." I sighed and looked around the restaurant to see if I saw her. Debo whistled and smiled holding his hand out to congratulate me. I still was processing this shit, but I slapped hands with him.

"CONGRATULATIONS, lucky ass nigga. Era good peoples. I vouch for her." I nodded my head. "But shit you got a situation at home, don't you?" I shook my head no.

"WE ARE DIVORCING it should be finalized in another month. She got pregnant by that nigga Dmack."

"GOOD THING I KILLED HIM." Debo crazy ass chuckled. "Nah on some real shit I hate to hear that shit my nigga. I got played by a scandalous bitch too in the worse way. I thought that shit was gon' leave me bitter towards females but then I fell for Praylah." Just as she spoke her name, she was sitting down with a plate piled with steak, shrimp, eggs, and grits. She blushed at him as he lifted his hand and caressed what looked like a purple and red birthmark on her cheek. The two started conversing as I picked up my phone and went straight to my group text messages with Sovereign and Roberto.

ME: meet me at the crib, it's important.

. . .

BERTO: I'm here in my new room, is it okay if I have company?

I FROWNED and shook my head. I thought this nigga was playing about picking out a new room at my new crib, but he wasn't. I texted him and told him hell no and he responded that I was boring. Sovereign hearted the message. She normally didn't respond; she wasn't good at texting, she normally called right away like she was doing now.

"WHAT'S UP SIS?" Sovereign always remained quiet the first couple of seconds on a phone call, even if she called you. She took her time at everything she did and thought out every word she spoke.

"WHAT'S GOING ON?" Her voice lacked emotion.

"NOTHING I just would rather tell y'all what's going on with me in person and at the same time, so I won't have to repeat anything."

"O-KAY. I'll be there in a hour." She hung up as I looked up at Debo who was now pecking Praylah on the lips. She walked away and he started stabbing his fork to the plate taste testing everything. When he ate a big amount of food, he wiped his mouth then started talking business.

. . .

"I WANT to create a paid season for hood players. They get a payout at the beginning and end of the season. We can have mini bowl rings like the super-bowl and cash them out that way it urges them to play hard for their families. I wish niggas with money had done shit like this back in the day. You know how many talented niggas there is in the hood that didn't get a chance to make it out? We can air it on TV and charge fifty dollars a ticket for the champion game and fifteen dollars for regular games. We also can give a hundred tickets for free for people that can't afford the shit. I figure we can start some shit how Ice Cube did with his own fantastic three basketball team. We invest fifty, fifty and split profits. You donate some and I will do the same." He picked his fork up like he didn't just come up with something extraordinary and started eating again.

I WAS SHOCKED because I remember when I played football in high school. I was so poor that I had to focus on providing for me and my sisters, so I stopped paying it any mind. If it wasn't for Sovereign and Inferno, I would still be out in the streets hustling so I looked at this as an opportunity to give back.

"I'M DOWN A HUNDRED PERCENT." That shit had me geeked and ready.

"GOOD, I'm glad you down. I'll have Alesia mail you all the paperwork to look over. Since we both be busy, we need to hire coaches and a good team to organize all events."

. . .

"I don't mind being a coach too." He nodded his head and picked up his cup of juice, downing the entire glass.

"That's even better. I plan to start this shit in two weeks. I don't want to waste any more time. I got a team; you just need to gather yours. A little promo on social media will help with that."

"Fully noted my nigga, I'm on it starting today. I appreciate the opportunity." We slapped hands again just as Era approached our table.

"Mr. Brownston, I'll be in touch. I thank you for everything." She didn't bother to look at me. But I cut right into the bullshit.

"Era, we gotta talk and we have to do it right now." She looked over at me and frowned.

"We don't have to do it now; we can do it later," she suggested, but I shook my head. I no longer had patience and barely had the pleasantries. All that being super nice to a woman got my heart broken so fuck it. I stood up and told Debo that I was getting ready to bounce.

"We gon' do that shit today, unless you want to do this shit here. I ain't did shit to you that you didn't accept. Now if you want to be on some adult shit, we can but if you keep acting like you got a pair of Huggies on then I'm gon' treat you as such." I gave her a stone expression and dared her to come back with some bullshit.

"LET'S ROLL." I walked ahead of her; I heard her say a couple nicer words to Debo as I made my way to the door. Holding the door open for her she walked by looking me square in the eyes. The air and wind around us seemed to hold a charge of electricity that I can't understand at the moment. She was pulling on everything inside of me like she was magnetic.

WATCHING the way her ass bounced with each profound step had me ready to peel that black romper off and slid deep inside of her. Everything flowed with Era, her thick hair, sweet scent, short shapely legs that I wanted to keep wrapped around my waist. Era was bad as fuck, and she knew that shit.

SINCE THE FIRST time I met her, it was hard to keep my balls from tightening. My dick was so fucking hard that it hard. Her presence made me forget about shit that I should be focused on.

"FOLLOW my truck all the way to my house. No funny shit Era, if you go the other way I'll just pull up to your location." She rolled her eyes hard and pulled her sunglasses over her scolding eyes.

. . .

"Whatever." She walked towards her car, and I watched that ass all the way until she was inside of her whip. I jumped in my Range Rover and headed towards my house. Life was just crazy as fuck. One moment I'm hurt over Jocelyn the next a chick that I didn't know turns up supposedly pregnant.

Thirty minutes later, after constantly looking in my rearview mirror to make sure Era was behind me. I used my access remote to enter my twenty-car garage. I parked and didn't open my door until Era parked right next to me.

The garage led me right into my home. I still couldn't believe Sovereign got me this big ass place. It had everything that I could think of to have the contractors add.

Since Era still had that mean look on her pretty face, I walked towards the door inside of my garage and it opened. The first room was the laundry room which was big enough to chill in. It had cushion seats and benches. With four washers and dryers, shelves with cleaning and different detergents. Luv spoiled ass had a tv put in claiming to want to watch movies while she washed then folded her clothes.

"I'm only here because-"

. . .

"YOU HAVE TO BE, and you will be, now let me introduce you to my family then we can have a conversation privately."

SHE SMACKED HER LIPS; I grabbed her hand and held it loving the feel of her soft hand in mine. This was too soon for her to even meet my people but shit what was too soon if she was already carrying my baby. To be real, if it were true, I wouldn't want to let Era out of my sight. I needed to feel her out more and get to really know the woman she was.

SINCE SOVEREIGN and Roberto were here, I felt like Era could sit in my conversation so she could understand where me and Jocelyn stood.

WALKING in my family room it felt like we were in a nail salon with all the fumes of nail polish and whatever else filling up the space. I spotted Roberto first doing Passion nails. I mean the nigga had a mini desk in my family room with all kinds of nail equipment laid out on top of the desk. He couldn't hear me and Era walk in because he had a nail drill going as they talked over the noise of the drill.

Making my way to them, Roberto stopped the grill and smiled.

"WHAT'S UP TOP SHELF BOOTY." Era giggled and so did Passion.

. . .

"TEDDY, look at my nails! Uncle Berto really hooks it up." She held her right hand up and smiled hard. I didn't too much care for Passion to have long nails, but she seemed obsessed with it, so I let it fly.

"YEAP and I'm next before you fly out Unc, I want mine done too." Luv walked in wearing some shorts that I didn't approve of with her stomach all out.

"WHERE'S SOVEREIGN?"

"IN THE KITCHEN on the phone and cooking." Roberto started the drill back up and went over Passion's nails. I couldn't lie he really had my sister shit looking like she went to the nail shop.

"I HOPE she ain't cooking nothing big. Inferno already stated that he ain't want her cooking for nobody but him." I chuckled but I was very serious. Inferno was a crazy ass nigga; he really was insane when it came to his wife.

"I NEED y'all to wrap that up I want y'all to meet a friend of mine. Era these are my two sisters Luv and Passion." I pointed to each one of my sisters and they greeted Era smiling and properly speaking like I taught them.

. . .

"I KNOW WHO SHE IS! Era aka Black Barbie oh my God me and Passion love listening to all your music. I'm so happy you getting the credit you deserve." Luv walked right over to Era, and they embraced each other like they were long lost friends. I never even witnessed Luv hug or interact with Jocelyn that way. I ain't gone lie that shit moved something inside of me and I was happy to see my sisters gush over a chick I possibly would end up with if shit worked out that way.

I hate it, I even ignored the red signs with Jocelyn. I felt like she didn't have to connect with my sisters because she wasn't their mother. I did expect her to create and have her own bond with them but that never came. Here was a total stranger standing in front of me talking and having a full conversation now about music and asking them questions to get to know them in front of me. Roberto even joked and joined the conversation and it all seemed to flow like they had all been close for years.

ERA WAS REALLY A COOL CHICK, she acted like she was super mad at me. I just appreciate that she didn't take her anger for me out on my family which was another big plus.

I TOOK a seat on the couch and waited for Sovereign to come in the room. I was waiting patiently for her because her opinion mattered a lot to me. She could read a person just from shaking their hand and saying a little to any words. She walked in looking beautiful with her wild messy curls all over her head. Sovereign's brown skin had a natural constant glow to it. Made a person wonder how she kept her skin so smooth and flawless. She was all about skin care and taking care of your skin. If it wasn't for her all the acne, I used to have would still be all over my face.

SHE MADE all the bumps and scars from picking at my bumps when I was a teen disappear. A nigga looked good now.

"I HAD TO MAKE SOME NACHOS-" she stopped talking abruptly when she saw Era. Everybody got silent trying to gauge Sovereign's mood. She got really quiet and observant when it came to strangers. Most of the time she opted out of speaking or even acknowledging a person's presence.

"OH, COMPANY?" I nodded my head and watched Sovereign sit the big tray of carne asada Nachos on the coffee table. She sat down on the couch and nodded her head at me.

"ERA THIS IS QUEEN, she's like a big sister to me. Queen, you met Era at my birthday dinner."

"Noted, nice to formally meet you... Era." She smiled quickly then focused on her nachos.

I RUBBED my hands together as Sovereign made eye contact with me. Speaking an unspoken language with her eyes. She had questions but probably wouldn't ask them until she and I were alone. I told everyone to sit around the coffee table so they could hear all that I had to say. Sovereign and Roberto were always busy, so I didn't burden them right away with everything, especially concerning Jocelyn. Luv was nosey so she knew a lot more than what I wanted her to know. She was basically happy that I was leaving Jocelyn, both the girls were happy with our new house and Jocelyn not being around.

SOULFUL HURTZ

"*H*ave her abort it. You don't even know the chick."

SOVEREIGN, Roberto and sat around the coffee table discussing my entire situation. Era stated that she didn't feel too good and needed to lay down, so I had Luv and Passion show her to my room and to get her some fluids just in case she threw up. My sisters were actually pumped about Era being pregnant. Sovereign stayed quiet the entire time and just listened to me talk and Era weighed in.

"SHE'S PRETTY; got a good head on her shoulders and I can tell she's not after the money. I just don't think it's the best for both of you guys. Considering the situation and the media wrapped up in both of you. As for Jocelyn, I can send my men to the house and have her thrown in Hades. Inferno has been wanting to burn shit up lately, that can be an early birthday gift for my man." She smirked looking at her witch shaped nails that were painted red, her husband's favorite color. The tips of her nails even had small orange flames traveling down.

SOVEREIGN WAS JUST as crazy as her husband. They were a match made from hell, but they really were good people and why I considered them family.

"I LIKE TOP SHELF BOOTY. I see some sort of chemistry for the two of you. Society thinks it's wrong to move on so fast when you just got out of a relationship, but I say…. Fuck society for that! I say… Go for what your mind tells you backed up by di heart." Roberto smiled and lit up a Cuban cigar.

"SAY'S the man who married a husband and a wife." Sovereign rolled her eyes.

"YES, you hear me say, fuck society. Who made all these morals and principles. People care too much about what others will think. I go and do what I want, no one's thoughts or opinions can stop me." Roberto stuck his nose up and smoothed his hair back.

"Era music career is starting to take off, you're in the media and got a lot of endorsements. Right now, they are talking about your divorce. It's bad enough they make assumptions about you having connections to Berto and his cartel in Mexico. You don't need too much attention Soulful. So, tell me, what is it that you want to do. What exactly are your plans?" Sovereign sat forward and put me right in the hot seat. She never wasted much time getting to the bottom of any solution to a problem.

"I WANT her to keep the baby, I want to get to know her as well. She's different, and I've been drawn to her since my birthday. I don't know, it sounds crazy but that's what I want." I cringed inside waiting for Sovereign to scold me but instead she just giggled smoothly and shook her head.

"I DON'T KNOW who stresses me more. My kids, you... or Berto's silly ass. You never answered my reference to Jocelyn? What are we doing about her?" Sovereign's eyes gleamed with hunger. I wouldn't dare suggest her letting Inferno burn my ex-wife alive. I still had love for her despite her disloyalty.

"LET HER BE QUEEN." I stated, sternly to make it clear that she wasn't to mess with Jocelyn.

"CHILLLEEEE, ju become football player and get soft overnight. I say chop that pussy off first since that's what she betrayed ju with." Roberto was always down for a kill as well. He was way more gruesome than Sovereign.

"LET HER BE, I still have love for her, and I will make sure she continues to be okay as long as she listens to what I told her. Just let her be for now."

. . .

"WHATEVER." They both said at the same time as Sovereign looked at her watch.

"I HAVE TO GET GOING, let the girls know I will bring the kids by Friday for them to babysit until Sunday." She stood up and I got up to walk her to the door. Her car and security were already waiting for her outside of my home. She turned toward me and gave me one of her famous speeches.

"I LOVE YOU TEDDY, proud of the man you have become. Your type of loyalty is commendable, some don't even deserve it. I'm rocking hard with you until my heart stops beating. Just make the best decisions and guard your heart a little better." I nodded my head and gave her a hug. When she pulled away and turned towards the steps my heart started pounding.

FEELING overwhelmed with a lot of emotions, my past and present started to rush me until I found myself standing outside of my door calling Sovereign's name.

"SOVEREIGN?" She stopped walking down the steps and turned towards me.

"YOU KNOW... my sisters, you and Berto plus this football shit is all I got. Y'all the only good things that has kept me going. I'm a man and we often don't get to express ourselves without society viewing us niggas as feminine or bitch made.

Jocelyn almost was my breaking point again. Felt like she took a hammer and shattered a niggas heart and soul like my momma did when she overdosed. I guess I was always holding on to hope with that lady thinking even if me, Luv and Passion would get older she would someday get clean and make us completely happy. Then she...she." I couldn't get the words out as my heart felt like it was splitting into two again. I never really got to express my feelings on my mom passing.

I JUST WENT about shit normally and tended to those around me. I put everything and everyone else first except my own feelings. My throat had a painful lump forming that was hard to swallow down. Sovereign embraced me right on the top step and I let out a cry that sounded like a Lion roaring out in pain from losing his pride. I remembered the third time my momma had got my hopes all high and shit promising me sobriety.

EYEING MY SISTERS WARILY, I got out of bed stomping my feet at the roaches that scattered upon realizing that there was movement. I woke up every morning at five am like my mind had a built-in alarm clock. Every day that I woke up, I felt more tired than before but had to keep pushing. Money had to be made and I had two mouths to feed. I stretched out the aches that I felt from sleeping in a small ass twin bed and yawned. I weighed about three hundred in some solid change. The bed I slept in was old from when I was five years old. I looked over at the bunk bed that my sisters were on and smiled a little bit. They were constant reminders of why I went so hard.

. . .

AFTER SHOWERING and handling the rest of my hygiene, I sluggishly made my way to our small roach-infested kitchen. I stopped in the living room and looked down at my mom on the couch with disgust. She had to get her ass up and fuckin' bounce before my sisters saw her and started crying and shouting. I hated her so much for what she put us all through but still loved her at the same time. Instead of starting the pancakes and bacon for my sisters, I decided to wake my mom and kick her out first. I knew with me cooking breakfast, the smell alone would wake my sisters up. I didn't want them starting their day off emotionally and still having to go to school.

I HAD to hustle hard and make moves, school and daycare for the girls was a life saver. It let me move around how I needed to during the day before turning it in early to take care of my siblings.

"ANTIONETTE." I shook her frail arm as I eyed her with disgust. "Antionette, get up man!" I raised my voice trying to sound strong and cold but what nigga wanted to see his mom strung out on crack? This shit a different type of pain and I wished my momma was strong and not weak when it came to getting on this shit. My father died when I was two, she met my sister's dad and shit started to spiral out of control. At the time I was eight and knew a change had come over my mom. She used to spoil me hard and tell me daily affirmations. When my sister's dad came into the picture, she became head over heels and lost focus of being a mother. My sister Luv

125

turned two, my mom was strung out and hoeing. She stopped caring that she even had kids and would leave us at home all day and night with no food or lights. By the time Luv turned three, she came home pregnant with Passion. She was so high off crack that when she delivered my second baby sister she laughed and told the nurses that she had a "Passion for crack." Cps got involved and gave custody to Passion's dad. That nigga was a stupid ass drug dealer that was constantly getting high on his own supply. I called him a functioning crack head. He didn't look like he smoked that shit but behind closed doors he shamelessly hit his pipe.

HE BEAT my momma ass constantly then threatened her to get clean so she could be a good mother and she complied and gained custody back over Luv and Passion and actually started doing what she was supposed to be doing. I was actually happy until a couple months later the nigga that Gerald owed re up money to, sent his goons to break down the door and capped his ass. At the time it was some traumatizing shit to see at a young age. Seeing blood and Gerald's eyes still opened horrified the fuck out of me.

I WAS happy that his ass was dead too though, and figured my mom would go back to being how she used to be before Gerald came into the picture, but I was wrong as fuck. Right after Gerald's funeral, my mom got high right in front of us when we returned back home. She received a big amount of money from the Victim of a Crime Organization and blew it all on drugs. When I turned fourteen, she stopped paying the rent on the house. That's when I realized that my mom never owned the house that we lived in and Watts. We got evicted and went straight to a women's and kids shelter until they gave her Section 8. We only lived in the shelter for three months and they gave her a voucher fast and that's when we moved into the projects.

FROM THAT POINT on everything was on me and I struggled up until I met Queen. At first, I hated her because I had to work off a debt. I stole from one of the niggas that lived next door to me. I was so hungry and weak, tired of hearing my sisters crying because they were hungry too. I didn't have no other options but to climb through Peep's window and take that nigga whole re up money. I knew he sold drugs and had it going on, I figured he wouldn't miss the money. When days went by without Peep saying anything to me. I thought I got away with it and shit was smooth.

A WEEK LATER, my front door was kicked in. Queen stood at my door with fire dancing in her hazel brown eyes and a gun clutched tight in her hand. When her eyes landed on me and my sisters sitting on our worn-down sofa, eating popcorn while watching The Simpsons. She handed Murk'um her gun and asked for his Gucci belt. She had the girls go to their rooms and whooped my ass with that Gucci belt all around the house until she was breathing heavy and out of breath. From that day forward, I worked off the debt and got to know her more.

INSTEAD OF LOOKING at her like an annoying ass boss, I started looking at her in a different light. I had to shake my thoughts of wishing she was my mom. She was full of wisdom and although everybody saw her for a cold, twisted and evil female. I saw her as more. She cared and she never looked at me with disgust or judgmental eyes. Niggas and females constantly made fun of me so much that I started believing the shit they said. It was all talk because I would never let a muthafucka physically hurt me.

I SHOULD HAVE BEAT niggas up and had a comeback for bitches that called me names. I had gotten used to verbal abuse at a younger age because of my mother. Whenever she didn't have drugs and whatever else she wanted, I suddenly became fat black and ugly niggas. That shit was the norm and at some point, I stopped giving an actual fuck. The only thing I truly cared about was making sure Luv and Passion had food on the table and warm decent clothes to wear.

I DIDN'T GET to experience shit that teens my age got to experience. I looked and felt like a grown ass man. I didn't want handouts and for people to look at a nigga and feel bad. I knew that one day because of my ambitions to get to the money, that the tables would turn.

I LOOKED DOWN at my mom and the same pain that I had been battling and trying my hardest to force out of my system when it came to her kept resurfacing. She had on a t-shirt that looked three sizes too big as drool seeped out the corner of her lips. Her ashen chocolate face looked like she was sleeping good as hell. My mom was beautiful even with sunken cheeks and yellow teeth.

. . .

"*WAKE UP MAN!*" *I shook her harder as she slowly stirred and simpered. Finally, batting her eyes and staring up at me in confusion, she sat up on the couch looking around the small living space. She smelled like dried up piss and from the heavy bags under her eyes, she hadn't slept in days while binging hard.*

"*SHIT, Soulful Hurtz! Why you bothering me this early?*" *I stood back from the pungent smell that hit the air and realized she had pee stains on her gray sweats.*

"*YOU GOT TO GO, Ma. I don't need the girls waking up for school seeing you.*"

MAINLY LUV, Luv was old enough to understand this shit clearer. She had anger problems and would act out for attention. Seeing my mom would make her not want to go to school just from fear of coming back home and not seeing her again. Passion was nonchalant and never really voiced how she felt but I could tell it bothered her.

"*WHY? I miss my babies and I want to cook for y'all tonight.*" *I shook my head and fought the urge to grab a cigarette from the kitchen cabinet. I hid them well so the girls wouldn't get curious and try to play with them. My mom stressed me so bad weed just wasn't enough. A roach ran across her foot, and she didn't even flinch to find out what was trekking across her foot. Looking at my mom in such a pitiful state pained me bad. My throat started to burn, and I hated the feeling of fighting back my own tears.*

"FUCK, Ma! You gotta stop doing this shit to us. We fuckin' love you and you don't give a fuck." I gritted as my bottom lip trembled. I didn't give a damn how weak I looked, I just wanted my mom back, I wanted her to be normal and if she couldn't be a mother to me, at least Luv and Passion deserved it. It was already too late in my case. What hurt me the most was seeing my sisters disappointed. Luv was nine years of age and Passion was seven.

"I CARE SOULFUL, that's why I keep coming back. I just need help and I've decided to kick this shit." I heard it before but looking into her glassy eyes made me feel like she was actually shameful. "I can't explain the feeling that shit gives momma, but I'm tired of how it's making things with my kids."

I SIGHED and ignored the horrid smell coming from her and sat down next to her. My heartbeat hard against my chest.

"HOW CAN I HELP YOU MA?" I would never give up on her even though I wanted to.

"YOU CAN'T HELP me Teddy, I gotta do it myself." I nodded as I continued to stare at her. If she didn't smell so strong, I would pull her in for a tight hug and never let her go.

. . .

"ALRIGHT MA, but you got to go. Luv gives me a very hard time. When you pop up and leave without saying shit, Luv's anger is a lot to deal with." My mom smiled and rolled her eyes.

"ALL SHE NEED IS her ass whooped, Teddy. You, always soft on them heifers."

"SHE NEEDS HER MOM, then a lot of the anger would go away." I reasoned.

"Y'ALL GONE HAVE ME, I think I'ma check into that rehab your aunt keeps telling me about. I'm really serious Teddy, I'm going to make up for everything-"

"MOMMY?" Luv rubbed her puffy eyes, ridding herself of eye boogers, and blinked a couple of times. Once she really focused and noticed that it was mom, she ran and jumped right into her arms.

"DAMN, MOMMY YOU STINK." She threw her arms around our mom's neck and kissed her all over the face.

"LUV, WATCH YOUR MOUTH." I scolded, but she ignored me like I wasn't in the same room. She did the normal inspection

and checked my mom out from head to toe. She talked to her about school and skipped subjects fast. Luv was breathing hard because she tried to talk fast to get it all out. I knew she did this because she didn't know when she would see our mom again.

LUV LED our mom to the bathroom to help her shower and pick clothes out for her. I took time out to go check on Passion. I knew if Luv was woken, that Passion had to be up and alert. When I walked into the room Passion was sitting up on the bed with tears in her eyes.

"WHAT'S WRONG P?" I hate seeing my sisters cry, it fucked with me in the worse way.

"I DON'T WANT her to see me." She sniffled.

"WHY NOT?" I sat next to her on the edge of the bed and picked her chin up with my index finger. Passion was beautiful with a nice kinky Afro. Most days I didn't know what to do to her hair, so I wet it and added leave-in conditioner. To top her fro off I would put different color ribbons and bows in it.

"SHE HATES ME, and she always leaves because of me." More crocodile tears came down her pretty round chocolate face. I pulled her close and rocked her in my arms.

. . .

"THAT SHIT AIN'T TRUE, P. Momma sick, she leaves to make sure she gets better."

"DOES SHE LOVE ME?" Her doe-shaped eyes were innocent the hurt behind them is what broke a nigga.

"OF COURSE, she love, loves you, she just don't know how to show it. She loves all of us and soon she's gone get better." I kissed her forehead and tried my best to reassure her. Although my mom should feel and see the effect, she had on all of us. I sat holding Passion, feeling like it was all my fault. After getting her calm and picking her clothes out for the day I went back to the living room and saw Luv and my mom sitting on the couch. I stood listening to their conversation.

"YOU GOT to get off those drugs mommy. Teddy doesn't cook like you and we be missing you." I wanted to laugh because I really couldn't cook for shit, but the girls ate whatever I provided because they didn't like being hungry. Luv was old enough to know what moms was on. Passion still went along with me telling her our mom was sick and I thought Luv still thought that too until now. She boldly expressed herself and I could tell from my mom's posture that she felt bad as hell.

"YOU LOOK GOOD NOW MOMMY. Those drugs make you look old, now you look like a hot girl." She snapped her fingers and smiled. She put too much gel in our mom's hair and had it in a loose ponytail. My mom had on black leggings, and

one of my big ass pro club shirts. I could smell the dove and baby magic lotion in the room.

"I LOOK LIKE A HOT GIRL, LUV?" My mom smiled.

"HELL YEA." Luv cooed with her bad ass. For once it felt like we were that one happy family that I envied from my peers at school. Shaking off the thought, I made a quick breakfast and got a little happier when Passion emerged from our bedroom to sit next to our mom and talk. Her voice was always low and very timid but to see my mom interacting with the girls. She wasn't high but I was sure within the next hour she would have that strong urge to get high. I just prayed this time around she fought it and brought her ass back home.

"AFTER ALL THAT getting our hopes up and shit, she failed us. She almost got raped in front of Passion which I still think fucked my sister up to this day. She almost got Luv raped then she couldn't seem to forgive herself for that stunt. She fell harder on drugs which crushed a nigga spirit even more. What broke me bad was her being selfish and never giving or showing me that me and her daughters was worth her really fighting her addiction and getting clean. Her ass went and died, Sovereign ain't that bout a bitch?" I wiped my face as Sovereign rubbed my chest. I could smell Roberto's perfume as he put his arms around Sovereign and pulled me along with him. My mind felt heavy, and my heart was bleeding out. My conscious kept telling me to let it all out and that's what I did.

· · ·

RENOVATING THE HEART OF A BEAST 2

I CARED TOO much like Roberto said. I didn't want to care at all about what outsiders or anyone thought of me. I gave shit my all and constantly tried to show fairness and realness. I always displayed my strength and led by example because I didn't want my sisters to ever think I was incapable. I wanted them to look up to me and see that I was going hard to give them the love that I never received. I think I fucked up worse by thinking that I can fill that love with Jocelyn. Its why I seemed to have a hard time getting her betrayal off of my mind and heart.

"I REALLY LOVED Jocelyn and then she let me all the way down with drugs. The same thing that killed my momma. I wasn't good enough for her or my moms and Jocelyn taking me through years of not knowing how it even felt to get affection from a bitch romantically only sexually and that was even barely there. I was always understanding. I wasn't some horny paid ass nigga forcing her to fuck me." Sovereign moved back and we all broke apart. Tears stained her and Roberto cheeks as she used her hands to wipe mine away.

"I WAS SCARED OF BREAKING; I swear I was so close to breaking. Then Era…. I don't know…"

"SHE CAME at the right time with the special remedy. Don't feel ashamed about that. You're reluctant with her because she's new. You feel some shit in your entire being like she's meant for you. Like God sent someone to help renovate all the things that has kept you down and under from destruction of others like your mom and Jocelyn. Follow it and just know that I know that it's real. I experienced that with my husband and I'm happy I didn't fight it. Both of y'all know all the disloyal shit I've been through from my own blood. I still regret not killing Empress when all she ever ended up doing in the end was killing herself with drugs and guilt. My relationship with my father is back like it was. I feel like I was better off thinking the nigga was dead." Sovereign blinked back more tears and quickly wiped them away.

WE ALL STOOD CLEANING our faces and wiping our tears away. This heart-to-heart moment made me feel like boulders were being removed from my shoulders. Sovereign dealt with a lot of heart ache. I witnessed her transform over the years and become a totally different woman. The hurt and betrayal that her family had caused her couldn't be survived by the strongest individual, yet she overcame that shit. That's why I always looked up to her and loved her like a big sister. She had my back since day one.

"OH MAN. I need to call my wife and husband for that chileeee. God sent me a double blessing and I'm out in these streets just playing around. I'm going to go shower and my room then call my pilot and tell him to gas the jet. I need to go home." Roberto wiped his face, pulled out a makeup compact mirror and eyed himself long and hard making sure he looked picture perfect. Next, his dramatic ass tossed his hair over his shoulders. Pulling his cellphone out of his hot pink shorts he walked into the house with the phone glued to his ear shutting the door behind him.

. . .

SOVEREIGN AND I looked at each other and doubled over in laughter. She eyed her security and frowned.

"I SHOULD FIRE Y'ALL." She smiled and patted my shoulder. "Teddy got me out here looking weak and shit." We both laughed again. I felt lightheaded from crying so hard. I didn't realize how bad I needed that shit. Hell, we all needed it.

"ALRIGHT, well you and your girl in there got some shit to discuss." We said our goodbyes and I headed back in to see Roberto sitting back at his small desk with nail supplies talking with Luv like he didn't just say he was leaving. They were so deep into their talking that they didn't even notice me pass them to go into the guest bathroom to clean my face up. I was ready to go have a talk with Era about what it was we needed to do moving forward.

ERA

$\mathcal{I}$ hated that I was so nosey, but I wanted to know more about Soulful. Sitting around his family and the way he broke down the whole situation between his wife and him, made me realize that we both had gotten hurt. When Sovereign asked for them to just talk alone, I respected that and left. It was perfect timing to retreat to Soulful's room because my stomach was back on ten and I was hugging his toilet throwing up.

It was not in my plans to snoop and listen to anything until I heard the front door opening. I went out onto his nice big balcony and sat down in the chair for air and that's when I heard him pouring his heart out. It crushed me and had me tearing up. I was so mean to him without even getting to know why he decided to even sleep with me. We both had the same feeling when it came to feeling connected and attracted to each other on the day that we met.

This entire situation had me feeling a little weighed down from all the what ifs. Finding out that Soulful was divorcing his wife had me feeling better about me sleeping with him. I didn't want to appear like a homewrecker or some side chick because I was not raised that way and I couldn't stand females who proudly slept with other women's men thinking that shit was cute because it was far from that.

When Soulful disappeared back in the house, I knew he was on his way up. I hurriedly went back into his room and laid across his king size bed like I was resting. His room smelled so manly and good, like the cologne that he wore. His room décor was dark forest green and black. I loved all the room that his private space had. If this was my room, I would never leave out of this space unless I had to.

Soulful walked in with squinted accusing eyes, it looked like he already had known that I had been listening in on his conversation. I wouldn't say anything about it if he didn't. Soulful was so massive in size. Very muscular and bulky, he had a little gut on him with a smooth brown baby face. His beard looked like he kept it oiled and his lineup was sharp and crispy with waves dipping in one direction. You can tell the man was paid but he had this super calm and humble aura about himself. He didn't let the money give him one of those snobbish fucked up attitudes and I was appreciative of that.

"Have you been to the doctor yet?" His brown eyes stared into mine. The fact that I knew he was just crying, and the evidence was clear from the red tint in his eyes, moved me to stand and walk up to him. My hands trembled because I wasn't that good when it came to this kind of thing.

"I kind of listened in on what you were outside talking about, I'm sorry for intruding into your privacy but I want to give you a hug. I hope that you also pray and give your burdens to God. It's okay to be vulnerable and in doubt some-times." I bit my bottom lip out of nervousness. This was the part when I was supposed to hug him. I kind of froze up and he sensed that I was a little reluctant. He pulled me into his big strong tatted arms and hugged me tight as I put my arms around his neck, struggling on my tippy toes to embrace his large frame.

He bent down allowing me to readjust and pull him in tighter. I let my fingers caress the back of his head and before I knew it, I started trailing kisses up and down his neck up to his cheek. He kissed all over my shoulders and neck as well, until our lips connected then our tongues started the conversation. I was so turned on by how tight he was holding on to me, his hands grabbed so much of my ass that it felt like he was lifting weight off my back.

I moaned while his tongue overpowered mine and got lost in the sensation of the feeling of Soulful hands roaming my body.

"You tryna get fucked, huh Era?" His deep ass voice had me moaning, eyes fluttering looking up into his deep set of eyes. "You my baby momma, so that means… I'm the only nigga that can fuck. Fuck you raw and uncut at that." He grinned wickedly making my pussy drip with each word he spoke.

"Tell me baby momma, is you tryna get fucked real good then I feed you and my baby afterwards so we can have a conversation about you being pregnant and all that other good shit." He slapped me hard on the top of my ass, making my shit jiggle. "All this muthafuckin' ass. Thick as fuck, pussy got to be thumpin' and wet by now, take this damn romper off so I can see how wet I got you." He leaned forward and licked the exposed part of my neck.

My hands moved like he was in control of them. I slipped out of my spaghetti straps and rolled the entire romper down, until it formed into a puddle at my ankles. I thanked God that I wore a matching black lace bra and panties, I felt hella sexy standing in front of him exposed. Soulful licked his thick cinnamon lips and let his eyes roam my entire body.

"Thick ass thighs, all that chocolate sexy ass skin. We gon' make a beautiful ass baby. What you think?" He walked behind me and unsnapped my bra, pushing it off and letting it fall right in front of me. My titties sprung free as I grabbed them up in my hands and nodded my head yes to his question. My body was already trembling at the feel of his rough fingertips tracing down my spine. Until he got to the top of my panties, he eased them off with little to no effort and I gladly stepped out of those too.

"I don't know about you, but I want to know everything about you." He came around to my front and got down on both knees. He kissed the bottom of my stomach then lifted it slightly to kiss the top of my mound. His hands never left my ass, as he stuck his nose right between my legs. I could feel him inhaling and exhaling getting a good sniff of my wet pussy. When he took his nose from between my legs, the tip of his nose glistened with my juices.

Soulful eyes were hooded and low as he continued to speak, for the first time he had me speechless. No man has ever had that ability to render me into no words.

"I want to know what you like and dislike, I ain't gon' push shit fast with you. It's all about pacing ourselves. Just know I'm gone treat you with respect and I expect the same Era." Swiping his thumb over his damp nose, he licked my remnants of juices off and smirked. I loved this man smile down to his crystal white perfect set of teeth. Soulful is moving slow as hell and the ache between my legs is growing fast. The hard throbbing of my clit makes me feel super desperate to feel and gain some form of relief. Standing to his feet, his eyes start roaming my body again like he doesn't know where he would like to start first.

I eye the huge bulge in his pants and flashes of the last time we were intimate becomes alive in my brain. His dark eyebrows dip slightly in the center as his eyes lift from my chest to my face making my stomach flutter.

"Era...Earlier the way you acted, unacceptable. Always communicate with me, I ain't one of those niggas that will lie or hide some shit just for some sort of easy gain. I'm always honest, even if what I might say ends up hurting your feelings." I arch an eyebrow at him thinking in the back of my mind that he was most likely full of shit. He had me standing here naked and wet as hell. He already had eased himself into getting some more pussy from me and I wanted to give it to him bad.

"Why did you pay for all my studio time and Shelby, when you don't even know me and you only got to fuck me once?" his eyes stayed lowered to my breast, squeezing that huge bulge in his boxers my mouth watered.

"When you sang at the restaurant, and I saw the passion and hunger inside of your eyes. I already had made up my mind that you didn't belong there. I also knew that Shelby could take you far. She's good at what she does, and she is a super solid friend to have. Back when I lived in the projects, I didn't have too much of anything but dreams that I knew I couldn't fulfil because of the hand that I had been dealt. Until I started hustling hard and meeting Sovereign. She gave me opportunities and chances that she didn't even have to give a nigga."

He walked past me and took a seat on the edge of his bed. Soulful was a deep individual, the way he looked right into my soul whenever he talked moved me in ways that I had never been moved in before.

His dark brown eyes bore into mine as I felt a chill run down my spine. I still have many more questions, but I keep getting sidetracked by the sight of him and how his eyes shamelessly take me in. It felt like just his eyes had penetrated me, I grew thirsty as I took a couple of bold steps his way. I stopped a couple of inches away then asked him another question.

"Did you think because you paid and helped me get to this point that you could control me. Like have me any time?" Soulful blinked at me, his gaze softening slightly, I like that he didn't waver or make his eyes look elsewhere.

"No offense, but I didn't plan on ever even reconnecting with you again until I saw you at the restaurant again. I planned on speaking to you and letting you go your way. Don't get what I'm saying and take it the wrong way Era. The pussy is the best I ever had. Still, I know I got some shit going with my own feelings. Your worth more than to be treated as some sort of rebound. The chemistry we shared on the first night had me shook. Like it was on some meant to be shit, so I told myself to stay away from you to try to keep my loyalty in check for my wife."

The truth slams into me like a truck as we both searched each other's eyes. That same sexual charge started hitting me all over again and before I knew it, I was standing right between his hairy ass legs. Breathing hard, I placed my hand on his muscular shoulders. He leaned to the right, beard tickling the top of my hand and kissed it.

"I was getting... mmm, Soulful." His warm mouth captured my left nipple, and he tugged at it soft then hard. Pulling both of my breasts together like he was squeezing a sandwich, he popped both nipples in his mouth at the same time and sucked on them hard then bit at both of them. My head fell back, mouth fell agape, these eyes of mine were now fluttering like I was under his special spell.

"Finish what you were saying Era." He popped both nipples back into his mouth and the way that he was sucking and licking on them had me fumbling over my words.

143

"I was... ummm, oooo shit! Getting over somebody too." I cooed and held onto his shoulders looking down at him, watching him intently as he made out with my hardened pebbled like nipples.

"We get over both of our exes together, while we get to know each other for our daughter that's growing in your stomach." He looked up at me as he slid his massive hands between my thighs. Splitting my wet lips, his fingers found my sex and he played in it like he was collecting all my juices to save for later.

My nipples and pussy began to tingle as I try my very best to catch and pace my breathing. His mouth latched onto my breast, drawing my nipples deep into his hot needy mouth. I keep picturing him sucking on my pussy the exact same way as my knees buckled and trembled. Soulful stood up and holds me still with his mouth still latched onto my titties.

My skin and every part on my body felt alive, small tingles all over my body like I was close to climaxing without any penetration. I started whimpering as Soulful ran his hands all over my bare skin and palms the other breast, he toyed with my right nipple as he gave the left all his tongue and mouth action. My mind comes alive with nasty thoughts, like sucking the skin off of his dick and tasting his nut at the back of my throat.

With one swift motion, Soulful lifted me up as his beard tickles the flesh of my breast. He lowered me onto the bed pressing me up against his fluffy pillows as he kept contact with my nipples still driving me insane. My pussy quivered and leaked for him, he nuzzled closer to me, and I ran my fingers through the waves of his head this time pulling a deep raspy moan from his throat that almost sounded like a harsh growl. The vibration of his voice sends a thrill to my pussy making it thump with need as my thighs twist together.

"Dammit Soulful." I cried out, he knew exactly what he was doing and Soulful wasn't in any kind of rush to stop. It was like he was taking his time to become well acquainted with my body and I feel like I'm close to exploding with juices leaking down the crack of my ass. I kept him pinned to my breast, opening my legs, and reaching down between them.

Sitting up, Soulful took his shirt off and I'm turned on by the tattoos on his arms and chest. His arms are fit, his body so bulky with a little bit of gut that I couldn't wait to rub all on when I pass out from cumming hard. Reaching between my thick thighs as he pulls his boxers down and off, I strum my swollen clit then let my hips move with my fingers, dipping my index and middle finger in and out of my pussy while my thumb gave my clit the attention it needed.

Feeling sexy and ready to get nasty as fuck with Soulful, I took my fingers out of my sopping wet center then trace them up to my nipples making sure to leave my juices smeared on each nipple. I suckle the rest into my mouth then dip my fingers back into my center. Soulful gets back between my legs and I see the thickest dick my eyes had ever landed on. It has to be about nine inches, but the width and girth is fat as hell. No wonder I was so sore the last time I laid down with him.

I sat up, he captured my nipple and sucked each one, making sure to get my juices off of them. Grabbing his dick with both of my hands I jacked and twisted it then lick around his thick mushroom tip, enjoying the taste of his precum. Soulful reached down between my legs just as I got the whole tip of his thick dip into my wet mouth. Dragging his thick, rough fingers down my soaking slit, I move my hips to chase his fingers.

I couldn't even help the helpless moans that spilled from my mouth right on to his dick. I look into his deep dark eyes that were filled with heavy lust and pop his dick right out of my mouth like a popsicle.

"Lay back baby, I need to taste you. I need that pussy more wet before I get up inside of you." I laid back slowly as his eyes searched mine. Situation himself between my legs, he thrusted my knees up and he spread me wide as hell.

"Pussy look like it ain't never been touched, wet as hell, that shit beautiful glistening Era. You want me to stretch that shit don't you?" I nodded my head, and he shook his head no at me.

"Yes, Soulful. I want you to stretch me the fuck out." I begged, feeling my pussy gush out more as he pulled my knees and legs further apart.

"I am baby but you gotta let me taste this pussy first. Can a nigga do that?" I nodded my head, and he eased down and came face to face with my needy sex.

He started at my tight asshole and darted his tongue in and out of it then dragged it right up to my clit as he suckled it just like he did my fucking nipples. Soon as his tongue entered me, I lost control and came all over his tongue. My body shook hard and lifted off the bed as he kept his nose on my clit and his tongue buried inside of my contracting center, I could literally hear this man drinking down my juices making me even more aroused while I'm cumming. My thoughts were crazy wondering how the fuck did this man wife have the nerve to even cheat on him.

After this, I knew I wouldn't want any other man inside of me or licking on my goods but Soulful.

"Get on all fours, I need that big ass booty in the air." I

get excited thinking that he is finally about to stuff my pussy with all that fat dick he has but Soulful is still not full of eating my pussy. What the hell was wrong with him? I thought, as I almost jumped out of my skin when he leaned in and swiped at me with his long tongue.

First, he thrusted his tongue hard against my clit, then he ran it between my pussy lips. Soulful laped at my juices then flicks the tip of his tongue upward until he was tickling my asshole. The feeling was so intense that I tried to pull away, but he stopped me by grabbing my wide thick hips and kept me pinned in place. He continued his assault, thrusting his tongue in and around my ass. I love this new feeling, getting my ass licked and played with was an entire new feeling that I think I was growing addicted to.

"You taste so fucking good baby." He grunted. "My dick feel like it's gone nut before it even gets inside of you." He kept at it, teasing my ass with his tongue lashing. He reached his hand forward and toyed with my clit building more and more pleasure inside of me until I grip the pillows to my face and moan loudly into them. My toes curled and my insides clamped and fluttered around nothing, wishing it was that thick long dick of his. For the first time, I wanted to literally beg and plead for Soulful's dick to stretch and tear me the hell apart. The need was building, he was making everything, I mean literally everything wet and damp on my entire body.

Pinning my sensitive pussy to his face, he started doing that gulping shit again. Like he was thirsty and in need of a drink. Soulful gulped my pussy down greedily with his thumb pressed against my tight asshole. I gushed all over his face and beard as it scuffed against my wet flesh and thighs. Soulful was so fucking nasty, he started purposely smearing it all around his face and my thighs making everything damp and sticky.

"Fuck baby, you making me nut." He grunted and that made me cum even harder. His fingers slide in between my wet folds, spreading my pussy lips as if he was trying to study and size me for his dick. I felt his tongue touch my clit, he trapped it with his thick lips, I ended up backing my ass into his face and Soulful started tongue fucking my ass again while slapping it hard making my shit ripple and shake all on his face.

Everything felt entirely too good, I kept telling myself to breathe but then he entered me, and the time seemed to stand still. I lost my voice and my will to breathe as he filled me up until there was no room for me or my pussy to breathe. My entire body shivered as he eased out halfway then slammed right back into me. Holding my lower back into his massive hands, he moved himself in and out of me as he controlled the way my ass slammed up against him.

"This pussy too fucking good Era. Tell me this my pussy." He grunted and spread my ass cheeks while he pushed in and out of me. I feel the cool spit drip from his mouth and into my ass. He pushed his index finger inside of my tight asshole and pushed in and out as he delivered death strokes to my pussy.

It felt like Soulful was moving his dick in a certain way that it felt too fucking good. Secret places inside of me was being reached and touched making me cry out and moan with tears wetting up his cotton pillowcases.

"I swear this pussy is all yours baby, nobody else's."

He smacked my ass as I hiss out from the sting, biting my bottom lip he picked up his pace, now it felt like he was super deep inside of my guts.

"Just like I'm killing this pussy, I'll kill a nigga if you ever let another hit this shit." I should be scared but my pussy gushed out in response. He just didn't know how he got me

148

feeling because if he even thought about giving this dick back to his ex-wife or any other bitch, I didn't just see myself taking the high road like I did with Devin. Nope! This was the kind of dick that would have me speeding to my momma house and grabbing her deuce deuce to shoot a nigga down for fucking playing with my emotions.

Soulful didn't know just how fucking good his dick and tongue made me feel. The way he took his time with my body and explored it. The way he had my eyes getting stuck from rolling back multiple times.

"When you break some shit, you buy that shit Era. When I fuck you, I own you. All of this." His hands caressed my ass as he dug even deeper. "And this." He grabbed my breast with his dick buried inside of me. "This pussy and everything else attached to you belongs to me and I'm gone take good care of all of you and the things you care for and want to do." He leaned forward and kissed the top of my back.

Soulful acted a fucking fool inside of me and I gained my courage and started fucking him back to show his ass just what I was working with. When we got done, we ordered food, changed sheets, fucked again then showered together and went another round in there. When got out his massive shower, dried off and got in the bed naked. I was sure that my chocolate skin would be ashy in the morning from not putting on lotion, but I didn't give a damn.

I rubbed my bare feet against Soulful's rugged rough feet then snuggled under his tall, massive ass and fell asleep with him holding me tight. I remember saying a silent prayer because this man had me already head over hills for him.

DEBO

I stared right into my steely gray eyes that had a speckle of red. I already knew this was a dream I couldn't escape just had to take the ride and enjoy. This was the only time my fear got the best of me. I was facing myself l, and this part of me was way taller and darker. I could smell the evilness rippling off of Debo. I could also see the disappointment and anger that I had been keeping locked away.

"You know what the fuck this is, don't you?" His voice sounded mechanical; with each word he spoke, it echoed, making everything inside of me become alert.

"It's the only fuckin' time you let a real nigga out to play bitch boy!" His eyes turned red forcing the gray out of them. Constantly those jaws clenched tight as I felt myself stand and come face to face with Debo.

"Ain't no bitch in my blood!" I defended.

"Matthew Michaels! Got bitch running all through him! I'm Debo! The one that gives you the fuckin' courage to put muthafuckas in they place nigga! Don't you ever forget it." I took in our surroundings, and we were inside of my old apartment. The one I got when I grew tired of my dad controlling

150

everything I did when I was a teenager. I hated how I was feeling, scared and too fucking weak. I feared what this nightmare would become of because usually when I had to face off with myself it got lethal.

"When you let me take control and run us, nigga how the fuck that turn out to be?" He looked at me and smiled sinisterly.

"Deadly, a lot of people died, and it fucked with a lot that I had going." My heart started beating hard as my mouth dried up at the people and places starting to pop up around us. It felt like we were in a Time Machine, lots of things that I had done in the past came playing out before my very eyes. A lot of the wicked shit felt like it wasn't me half the time it wasn't. Debo had taken over whenever my anger got the best of me. I was never able to stop him.

"As it should be nigga. I'm a forced to be reckoned with a god and muthafuckas will respect the grounds I walk on." He turned away from me causing me to look down at the carpet. The smell of dead bodies and blood reeked making me want to throw up. Each step he took towards a woman who sat naked and tied up with razor cuts up and down her body had me ready to start fighting up out of this state of mind I was locked into.

A nigga appeared on the ground crying as my younger homies from back in the day stood around with hunger and lust evident in their eyes. Another me popped up next to Debo with a rifle in his bloody hands. He started yelling at the nigga that I now remember as Blade. Blade did some foul shit and had to pay. He offed a couple of my homies and Debo raged so hard that he took over for weeks and had me feeling like I couldn't snap out of anything.

I remember him ignoring every call from my siblings, mother, and father. It was the first time that I became super disgusted with myself and actually caused so much self-harm. For a while I was in denial about myself and the fucked up shit that I sort of felt like wasn't real. I didn't know how to sort that fucked up voice that felt alive out of my mental. I had my times where I would zone out. I had my times when I had dreams like the one I was having now and pushed myself out. I think the biggest thing was me not wanting to accept back then that I was really crazy.

My mom started mixing and making me good slushies that Ms. Scott told her about. All along those drinks had my medicines inside and it would help stop these way-out episodes and hallucinations that I would have. My mother noticed it before my father did. I would go to sleep and wake up in the living room fucking shit up. After all the beef and problems that I had with my sister's husband Ream. I thought I got the shit under control. Debo's voice disappeared and I thought I was fine.

It wasn't until months ago that I really realized something was back fucked up with me. I started handling business differently and looking at Ream and Solo like they were enemies although deep down, I knew that they weren't. When Debo started suggesting to kill Ream and Solo, because they were enemies. I started staying away from them niggas because I felt myself doing some shit that I would regret.

The person that meant the most to me was my father and mother. I had to stay away from them too. Half the time when they said shit that voice fucked with me the hard way and would say crazy shit about the two main people that I never wanted to hurt.

The scene played out live in front of me watching multiple men violate Blades wife in front of him. He cried and begged for it to stop as tears flooded my eyes. I watch the young me become so excited, cloaked in nothing but evilness. I started *slapping myself in the face and searching for something to knock me back into reality, but I found nothing. Debo voice started driving me insane as the tears start running down my face like a broken fountain. I wanted out but there seemed to be no escape.*

"Stop running from who the fuck you are! It ain't enough legal franchises you can make or buy to stop what the fucking program is nigga! You starting to let niggas walk all over yo' punk ass and it's making me look weak! Planning all this dumb shit and worried bout restaurants when we belong in the fucking streets!" Debo yanked me up and I fell limp and motionless in his strong arms. The worse feeling was feeling like I couldn't fight myself back.

"When niggas disrespect! This is what the fuck happens." He forced me to watch the young me pick up the gun and aim it at Blade's wife head. Without a second thought he cocked the gun and made her head explode as Blade screamed out loud in agony. Young Debo yelled for them to bring Blade's mom in, and I somehow found my strength to start fighting back. Until I saw Praylah on the side of me pulling me away from Debo. In a strange way, Debo had a look of remorse in his eyes. He turned me lose and when he did the blood from the carpet and the smell of dead bodies disappeared. The whole scene vanished, and everything turned dark.

I stood breathing hard with Praylah eyeing me suspiciously. I couldn't really look her in the eyes because I felt and knew for a fact that I looked insane to her. I was standing in my boxers, my white beater ripped up and tore. She rubbed my arm and when I finally looked at her, I noticed the phone glued in her hands with the number nine-one-one dialed, but she hadn't sent the call.

"Michael, you have to take your medicine love." Sweat

was evident on her pretty chubby face. She looked pale like she saw a ghost.

"You ruined your room and started throwing things in here." I looked around my living room and felt like a maniac. My glass table was shattered a couple pictures knocked off the wall. I didn't even want to see the damage that I had caused in my actual room. Clearing my throat and still trying to catch my breath. Praylah grabbed my hand and led me down the hallway in nothing but her panties and baby tee. I watched her thighs shake with each step she took causing her booty to move.

We got down the hallway and I stopped her midway to pull her in for a hug and kiss. I still was feeling misplaced and lost but I needed to feel her and love on her in order to bring myself some sort of sanity in this moment. *The only fuckin medicine you need.* I dug my hands in her kinky hair and kissed her deeper before pulling away leaving her panting hard.

"Don't ever call the police when I have one of those kinds of attacks. Just let a nigga be." I looked down at her short frame as she shook her head.

"Michael...you umm... were really hurting yourself, I didn't know what to do. You were pleading and begging to be let free. You kept screaming and it hurt me to see you crying and helpless." I touched my face, and the proof was there. My entire face was drenched, and my eyes felt heavy like I had been crying. Images of what I just experienced kept flashing all around us as I kept blinking hard and begging myself to let it go away. I desperately needed to go get a hold of my medicine, I feared scaring Praylah away. Ignoring what she just said to me, I wiped my face and continued down the hallway towards my bedroom to get my medicine and roll me up some weed.

"What time is it?" I asked looking back at her, it should have been a crime how thick and sexy Praylah was. It was hard to just look in her eyes when she had full perky big breast and big thighs and ass to match. You could literally look at her from the front and tell that she was toting some heavy ass shit behind her.

"It's seven o' clock, I'm already running late for the party." She fake pouted, then today came running back across my memory. Today was Honor's birthday, I wired her some money and had Johny Boy, our jeweler, send her some fly ass pieces to her house this morning. Honor started hanging with Praylah and her girls tougher when she wasn't caught up in the streets. She even became tight with Soulful's gay brother or homie Roberto. I wasn't up for making and hanging with a bunch of females, so I let her do her thing.

Tonight, she was supposed to have a big ass party at Ream's strip club. I thought about surprising her and just saying fuck it and go. Since my brain was super fried right now, I thought against it. I didn't need to go out and end up flipping the fuck out on people because somebody said or did the wrong shit.

"How you running late when that shit don't start until ten?" I looked at her walk off towards my bathroom and had to thank God that I had her here with me. Praylah and I had started growing closer the past couple of weeks. She thought I needed space and would try to give me that during her work weeks and I tried to respect that shit. It was hard because when she wasn't here with me, I found myself staying glued on the phone with her, listening to her every move, including her cooking, and interacting with Heaven.

I thought about the episode I just had and knew it set me back from meeting and spending time with Heaven. Praylah moved around my room with ease, she was very familiar with my house. She got me a cold bottle of water and walked back up to me with three pills in the palm of her hand. With her, I didn't feel like she was judging me, she was actually showing eagerness to help.

"This shit really gone have you making me wait to meet Heaven huh?" I put all three pills in my mouth and chased them down with water. Praylah didn't like when I chewed the pills, so I took them the right way instead of doing them how I normally did.

"Well, that was scary. Heaven never sees me act like that and I don't want her thinking That I'm putting her in another abusive situation. She is still young and moldable. I can make her forget about all the times Jarei put his hands on me in front of her because she is still young." My jaw clenched as my anger flared at the mention of that nigga. *That's why I have to remind you who the fuck you are!!! You should have killed him when you had the chance! All he's going to do now is show you how much of a pussy you are!* I shook my head like I was trying to shake that voice right out of my head.

"Michael." I looked up at Praylah and hated the way she was now looking at me. She looked like she was nervous and fearful to be around me right now.

"I don't mean it in a bad way, I just think you we should continue to take things slow with us before we involve Heaven into this." I solemnly nodded my head. Taking a seat on my side of the bed, I started thinking about how on edge I was again. This shit was frustrating as fuck.

I hated being off all this medication just to try to control the voices and hallucinations that happened every now and then. Though I trained myself to stop caring how the fuck people viewed me, I got tired of seeming so crazy and not being able to get a good enough control over it. I didn't even know why I was so caught up on Praylah, but that shit was starting to blow me to. Probably because I got tired of having that fear of losing her when I haven't even known her for the past six months. My heart beats differently when it comes to her and that was a red flag to me.

Her having that kind of control meant she would have me stepping out of character in the worse way. I didn't want to be anyone's burden, not even my parents. I didn't want people feeling like they needed to keep an eye on me because I was grown and could hold my own.

I yawned hard and felt a wave of sleepiness.

"I understand sugar mommy, I respect you for that too. I ain't stable enough to be around baby girl. When I do get to meet and be around her, I want her to view me as a hero. I feel and know that I gotta get better control over the shit I'm going through with my mental. Praylah, you gotta know this shit so hard baby. Shit is starting to break a nigga. The things...." I paused feeling my throat burn and that voice rage again. (Don't you dare say shit about our business! Pussy ass gone chase her away. She a green bitch! Keep it that way!)

Blinking my eyes hard, I felt myself ready to spazz out on myself.

"FUCK!!!! Shut the fuck up!!!" I used my fist to hit the center of my forehead! "Just shut the fuck up and let me talk got dammit!" I grabbed each side of my face and leaned down on my knees not even bothering to look at Pray. Like a magnet she slowly walked up to me and talked soothingly as she massaged my shoulders. I felt tired, like really fucking sleepy.

"I've done some evil thing that I'm not proud of Praylah. So, you see, I blame myself for ever letting something that's not real but just a voice control me."

"Nigga I'm real as fuck, and you betta be glad my bitch standing here. I know all your fucking fears nigga!" I looked around past Praylah and jumped at the sight of Debo standing behind Praylah with those red glowing eyes looking like he was ready to kill. He balled his fist tight, and blood started seeping out of his knuckles. That fear clutched onto me like a vice grip as I leaned away from Pray and talked directly to Debo.

"You ain't fucking real!" I stood pushing her to the side.

"That bitch Ms. Scott got you thinking that shit! That's why you should have killed her in that last session like I told you pussy boy!" He chuckled making my ear drums hurt.

"I do what the fuck I want!" I hit my chest as Praylah stepped back in front of me.

"Michael talk to me baby, are you seeing something in the room." She physically turned around to look around the room then back at me confused.

"Baby it's just your mind, nothing is there. It's only your mind." She repeated as I gave Debo a crooked smile.

"See nigga! You ain't fucking real!" I stomped away with Praylah following closely behind. Debo disappeared but he was loud and clear inside of my mind. *I'm very real to you, nigga, don't let that bitch confuse you. It was me that even attracted her to us! You know I'm real and you know what the fuck I'm capable of!* My body felt like it was trembling with anger as I walked into my bathroom to see what pills Praylah had given me. On the bathroom counter sat the three pill bottles. One of them was the wrong damn medication. It was my sleeping pills that would have me knocked out soon.

"Damn baby you gave me the wrong shit. Now this nigga gone really fuck with me in my sleep." I turned away from the counter and looked into her pretty ass face calmly.

"I'm sorry baby, I was rushing trying to get you your medicine and-"

"It's okay baby. Just get your things and go get dressed

somewhere else before you go out. I hired more security to go follow behind y'all tonight so you will be safe." I thought about that bitch ass nigga Sosa. Although I knew he wouldn't try shit. I still had to be thoughtful of Praylah's safety. I wanted to go and fight my sleep but the medicine that I just took would have me out very soon. I also knew that I wasn't even myself. I didn't want Praylah seeing anymore crazy shit from me.

"I don't want to leave you." She walked up to me grabbing at my eight pack. The feeling of her delicate hands had me wishing that my dick could get hard. I knew that was a no go because certain pills took away the ability to nut or sometimes get hard. I kissed her on the forehead then nose.

"Don't do that Praylah. I'm not a kid and this ain't my first go round with that voice babe. I got to fight this shit. I'll be alright trust me I always am. Think about all the nights you ain't here. I really be good it's not bad all the time." I walked back into my room and got back into the bed feeling myself close to dosing off.

"Don't go out wearing no tight ass shit showing off all that ass and thickness sugar mommy" I smiled trying to make light of the entire situation. The longer I stared at her the heavier my eyes got. The mess in my room, Praylah's face and everything else started to get blurry before I dosed all the way off in a world full of hell.

I WOKE up choking and coughing off of smoke. Panic set in my chest wondering just how far I went trying to get out of my nightmare until I heard an unfamiliar voice.

"Big B, put that shit out." I froze and wondered who the fuck was in my smoke-filled room. The lights cut on and so did my ceiling fan. My body was drenched as I coughed violently, desperately trying to catch a fresh breath of air.

"It's four thirty in the morning Debo. I'm here for answers and I don't bullshit, nor do I play around. The only reason you're still sitting up in bed looking confused as fuck is because your friend whose birthday it was is in the hospital clinging for her life. I'm not really a sympathetic nigga." He cleared his throat and finally I could see a clear view of him dressed in all red. His blue eyes were rimmed with redness like he had either been smoking or crying. I didn't really give a fuck what it was. All I heard was that Honor had been shot and was clinging to life. I reached under my pillow as he grabbed something on the side of him. It came into clear view, and I noted that this crazy nigga had a flamethrower.

"There's no gun under there. See, you seemed to be a troubled man. I've watched you toss and turn. Even cry hard as fuck. The whole time you battled and fought in your sleep. Big B found all your hiding places. Then I really got the chance to realize who you were associated with. The Blue Diamond Dynasty. Because I have respect for Ream, I'm giving you a chance to give me what the fuck I want. I'm a man with little to any time or patience." He smiled wide just as I met him with a frown.

"What the fuck you want?"

"The nigga that got my brother laid up in a coma. I know you're connected to Praylah who seems to also be missing in action. She was seen leaving out the back door with a nigga by the name of Sosa. My brother Roberto is a very important man, in the next two hours his golden triangle will want answers. I will not let the cartel step onto U.S soil in revenge for my brother when he has me his big brother that will solve and annihilate any problem. If the cartel comes here, then it's bad for my syndicate as well as the Blue Diamond Dynasty."

A million emotions hit me at once, first Honor now Praylah leaving with this nigga Sosa like she was okay with what all happened. I looked back at the blue-eyed devil as he stood up. A big nigga that he referred to as Big B gave me a murderous glare and went to stand by the door as a soft tap at my room door could be heard. A beautiful dark skin woman that I heard all about by the name of Queen walked in with an emotionless face. She was a Queen-pin a cold ass ruthless bitch that I used to crush hard on.

"It's nice to see that you have met my husband Inferno. I know you know who I am as well." She was dressed in all red matching her husband except she wore red leather pants with a crop top red shirt. Her red leather jacket stopped right at her waist showcasing her curves.

"Baby we need to get to the hospital." Inferno nodded his head and went right to his wife.

"Twenty-four hours. I want Sosa alive and breathing. If my brother doesn't survive then neither will you or anything you love."

To be continued …

Make sure to leave a review on amazon!

KEEP IN TOUCH

Subscribe

Interested in keeping up with more of my releases? To be notified first of all my upcoming releases and sneak peeks, please subscribe to my mailing list! https://bit.ly/3AYIwMK
   Contact me on any of my social media handles as well!
   Facebook- Authoress Masterpiece & Masterpiece Reads
   Facebook private group for updates- Masterpiece Readers
   Instagram- authoress_masterpiece & masterpiece_lgee
   Email – masterpiece3541@outlook.com

Made in United States
North Haven, CT
24 January 2024

47870907R00104